ISLAND OF
DREAMS

Eddie McCann

A story of love, treachery and
revenge –

A vivid portrayal of one man's
struggle for survival on a remote
South Pacific Island.

Island of Dreams

Copyright © Eddie McCann

ISBN: 1 903607 54 X

Typesetting and publication by:

Able Publishing
13 Station Road
Knebworth
Hertfordshire
SG3 6AP

www.ablepublishing.co.uk
email: books@ablepublishing.co.uk

Tel: (01438) 812320 / 814316
Fax: (01438) 815232

The author is a retired lorry driver living in Clifton on the outskirts of Nottingham. He served with the Black Watch in Kenya and spent some time in the South Pacific, which inspired this novel.

CONTENTS

CHAPTER ONE

THE VISITOR

Elizabeth Argyll looks older than her fifty years and is going blind, and when she decided to isolate herself from the world she couldn't have chosen a more remote spot to escape humanity. For the past fifteen years she has lived on Pago Mara, a South Sea Island in the middle of nowhere. Almost forgotten, seldom visited, she is the only white woman. Her home, a canvas lean-to, with hammock, chairs, table and unit stacked high with books, is reached up a alligator-infested river and a two-hour trek into the interior.

*****

She lives contently and totally alone. In her off days she is buoyed up by her memories. Her books and radio, her only contact with the outside world, get boring after a time. She grows vegetables, keeps her tiny settlement clear of the encroaching rainforest, and for company keeps dogs, cats, goats, chickens and a leopard cub until its mother came to reclaim it. Once a month a man from the village brings what she can't grow herself, and luxuries like tobacco, magazines and batteries for the radio, also a native boy drops round now and then to do jobs she can't do herself. She has a working knowledge of the local language so communication isn't difficult. One time she was attacked by one of the boys who was drunk. She didn't report it. She views it philosophically as something she has to put up with, one of the risks of living alone. "No one put a gun to my head," she says. Her stoic acceptance of 'what will be will be,' forms the fulcrum from which she gathers her strength.

*****

At night she lies in her hammock with her dogs around her, the goats tethered outside and the cats and chickens among the trees. Music from the radio lulls her to sleep. When she can't sleep a paperback whiles away the hours. With no deadline to meet, she can sleep when the mood takes her.

She has a routine and sticks to it. A wash in a nearby stream in the morning, breakfast, exercise the dogs and then tunes into the local radio station. If it's in English she takes special care to get the right channel. If not, she listens to phone-ins in the various dialects and amuses herself by comparing the varying pitch and cadence. Japanese is completely beyond her though she likes the music.

*****

Over the years she has never been embittered in her solitude although, as she puts it, it was bitterness that drove her there in the first place. A broken love affair shattered her illusions and taught her that love is the strongest emotion and can never be requited. "You always want more, more than you can give. If you dwell on what might have been you might as well curl up and die. You must look out of yourself, at the trees, flowers, animals, each with their own problems and each determined to get on with their lives. If you try to understand, it makes life that much easier."

But nothing lasts forever, not even solitude, no matter what lengths are taken to achieve it. Like everything else solitude has its price. Times catches up; times disguised as progress. The eco-system of the rainforest is threatened. Bulldozers have moved in flattering everything that gets in their way. Nothing is spared. You either move on or die. A bush pig and her brood seeking refuge have moved to the edge of the settlement, and there is nothing Elizabeth can do. She is as unsure as the future as they are. Chain saws are not sweet music. The twentieth-century and all it stands for, once only heard from across the ocean, is knocking on her door.

She has no place to go nor the strength nor will to resist, so setting up camp somewhere else is out of the question. It is her home and where she wants to be. "Mine is a melancholy and tolerable existence," she said. "Compared to a city it is less risky and not so unpredictable. In a city you can be murdered in your bed or die under a bus. Here, there is only one way I can go and it is where I belong. If they find my body I'll get a Christian burial. If not," she snapped her fingers, "the jungle will have me."

She spoke without rancour though her voice was tinged with regret. "If only the logging companies knew what they were doing," she cried. "Animals can't talk or write to the newspapers. When their habitat is destroyed where do they go, the sea? Even that's not safe. Drift nets and those bloody countries that hunt whales are emptying the oceans faster than nature can fill them. They say furniture and paper are recycled. Recycled from what? They've got to have the original in the first place. Trees are ripped up so that fat cats can sit at mahogany tables. Profit, profit and more profit. The loggers have been here three months. Three months too long. I hear they're having difficulty getting the trees off the island. Let's hope I'm right."

*****

The project she refers to is the conversion of vast tracts of forest to orange groves and coffee plantations to provide work for the natives of neighbouring islands who lost their rainforest years ago and can no longer grow crops because the land is barren after the top soil was blown into the sea. Then she spoke about her background and what led her to shut herself off from the world.

"A love affair?" I asked.

She sighed. "You could call it that. Not very original, I'm afraid. Half the convents and mental institutions are filled with women who were jilted at the altar or left holding the baby. It would have been easier if either had happened to me. No such luck. I fell in love. Leastways, I thought it was love. I'm not meant to have it the easy way. I always lose out. I've had my heartbreak and in a way have never got over it. I still cry in my sleep." She wiped away a tear. "Now I'm feeling sorry for myself. What must you think of me? You haven't come halfway round the world to listen to my belly-aching."

"I don't mind," I said. "I might learn something."

A smile passed over her face and it was easy to see she had once been beautiful. "You won't learn a great deal, I'm afraid, except how to be as miserable than I am. I'm sure you have other things to do. Why did you come?" she asked.

I told the truth. "To get your story."

"You've travelled far."

"I'm not complaining."

She was both flattered and startled. "Am I that important?"

"Someone thinks you are."

She sat down primly and arranged her dress that belonged to a bygone age. "I was what you might call a strange girl," she began. "A loner by nature and solitary to the point of seclusion. It's not that I can't mix with people as won't. People bore me. If I bore them they're too polite to say so."

As she continued it became clear she was painfully aware that she was different and it would always be a source of embarrassment. Perhaps that is why she came to these islands, to be alone. But there was more to it than that. I listened, and in a way wasn't surprised at what I heard.

At the age of seven she taught herself to read and write, and by the time she was fourteen she was fluent in four languages. She was an only child. Her father was a captain in the British army and took his wife and daughter to wherever he was posted. He died in Belize and Elizabeth and her mother returned to Britain. With no income except a meagre pension, Elizabeth's mother committed suicide. Restless and unable to settle, Elizabeth returned to Belize and from there went to New York where she worked in a department store. It wasn't long, however, before she got itchy feet again, going to places as far apart as Helsinki and Shanghai in search of happiness until finally she returned to South America, this time Mexico.

*****

"It was there I met Pedro," she said. "He worked in a nightclub; singer, dancer, all round entertainer. I fell for him like a ton of bricks. He was charming and knew the right things to say. When he proposed marriage, I accepted without hesitation, flattered that his feelings ran so deep. Though I wasn't so sure about my own feelings. All I knew was I was tired of moving from place to place and wanted a place of my own. The date was fixed for the wedding. I met his family and wrote to my cousin in Cornwall, the only living relative I had. Although we hadn't seen each other in years, I felt I had to tell somebody. To a shy, young woman marriage is the most important thing in the world even if no one I knew would be there. I was a bride-to-be with no family and no past. Pedro was too superficial to understand losing one's parents and travelling the world in search of happiness." She sighed. "Just when I thought I had found it I realised my mistake. It took me weeks of explaining why we should call it off. Pedro and his family were far from pleased. Cancellation was costly. The church organist demanded his fee, the caterers sued for compensation for a reception they didn't prepare and the organisers refused to refund the money. There were bad feelings all around. Pedro's family never forgave me. I heard he died of a broken heart." She laughed. "Too much tequila more like it. I left Mexico and finished up in Scotland."

*****

Getting to her feet, she went outside, put a can of water on the fire and came back. "I'll make a pot of tea," she said. "A twig in the water repels the smoke otherwise it tastes awful. A trick I picked up in the Girl Guides." She resumed her seat and continued, "I got a job and settled into a life of sorts, so different from what I was used to. The weather for one thing, cold, very cold, though the mountains were beautiful, capped with snow, a beauty all their own." She savoured the memory. "I got lodgings in a small town in the Highlands. One night I went to a party with friends, and then it happened. All the clichés about love at first sight and 'across a crowded room' came to mean something. I met the only man I would ever love. Not at all like Pedro - bigger, broader, quite the opposite really. I looked into his eyes and knew he felt the same. I went back to my friends in a daze. They thought I was drunk. I made my excuses and left but not before arranging to see him the next day."

I watched her make the tea. She passed me an enamel mug. I put it down quickly and blew on my hand.

She laughed again. "Hot, hey? I should have warned you. Pot cups are easily broken and tin mugs taste of metal. Enamel is neither but retains the heat." She shrugged. "You can't have everything. When you opt for a life like mine you take the rough with the smooth. No china or silverware here. You get used to it. Want to hear more?"

I was too hot to say anything. She passed me a damp cloth to wipe my neck and face. Sweat poured off me. The lean-to was like a furnace. It was mid-day and at its hottest.

"It's worse outside," she continued. "This is about as cool as you can get. The dogs are sheltering in the shade and the cats don't seem to mind. Goats adapt to all kinds of weather and the chickens - Well, chickens are chickens. They are all free to leave and fend for themselves but why should they? We are one big happy family." She smiled sweetly. "If you want to be on your way I won't mind."

"I'll stay a while if it's all right with you," I said.

The smile lingered at the corners of her mouth. She rolled a cigarette, struck a match, lit it, inhaled deeply, coughed and pulled a face. "Filthy habit I know but it makes life tolerable. It relaxes me and stops me reflecting on what might have been. I tend to dwell on the past and feel sorry for myself, although I can't say I haven't had my moments. Trouble is they're buried under mountains of regret. Where was I?"

"You arranged to meet him the next day," I reminded her.

She wrinkled her brow in thought. "Oh yes. We spent an idyllic afternoon on the banks of a river. The sun was shining and the mountains stretched as far as the eye can see. I was with the man I loved, what more could I ask for? If there is a heaven, that was it. Fate had been kind to me. Nothing could go wrong. He consumed me totally. I couldn't eat, sleep, but my God I was happy. We saw each other whenever we could and in no time we were lovers. We put our thoughts in a diary." Her face set in rigid lines of anger. "Then I found out he was married. I was heartbroken. There I was besotted with a man I would do anything for and all the time he was sleeping with another woman." The silence was resonant of the rustling leaves. "He used to write poetry," she added. "Would you like to hear some?"

I nodded.

She began in a voice both soothing and caressing. "I fell for your charms …And my arms held you tight," then studied my reaction. "Gushy you might say, but nice. There are three verses in all. I have them written down somewhere. He wanted to be a full-time writer, and contributed occasionally to the local newspaper. He was an incurable romantic. We used to hold hands and laugh, and he would chase me and I would stumble

14

and let him catch me, and then we would kiss." She drew herself and vented her feelings further. "Wife! Piffle! If she had been a wife he wouldn't have loved me the way he did." She calmed down and there was a twinkle in her eye. "But I got the last laugh. If only she had known."

I cleared my throat. "Did he tell you he loved you?" I asked.

She chuckled at life's cruel joke. "A thousand times but he would never leave her. I left Scotland and went on my wanderings again. Years later I was told she had died. I was tempted to look him up, to see if he felt the same but I didn't want another rejection."

I asked his name.

"Stewart Irvine," she replied. "Stewart to his friends and family. Irvie to me." She scanned a distant horizon. "It seems like only yesterday. Sometimes I wonder if he's still alive. But, of course, I know he is. I know in my heart. It would be nice to see him again if only to say hello. But people change. I don't imagine he would want anything to do with me now. I was young and pretty then. Look at me now"

"We all get old," I told her. "I bet he's no oil-painting himself if he's still around."

"He's around," she assured me. "So near I can reach out and touch him. I'll know when he's no longer with me. He's part of me. I touched the stars and for that I'm grateful. I doubt if I ever had that effect on him." She dabbed her eyes with a handkerchief. "That smile and those eyes. I'll never forget those eyes. If only he had known."

"Perhaps he did," I murmured, "but at the time could do nothing about it. By the time he could you were on your travels again."

She disagreed. "Nice thought but I don't think so. He wouldn't have left her. He had strong views on marriage. Catholics usually do."

I didn't tell her that even Catholics leave their spouses.

"They don't believe in divorce," she added.

"But it's not against the law," I argued. "Catholics have been known to divorce. Sometimes they have no choice."

"Practising Catholics don't."

I didn't press the point.

*****

There was a commotion outside. The dogs had a leopard trapped up a tree. They were snapping and growling as they circled the trunk while the leopard bristled and spat. It flicked its tail from side to side, measuring the distance for a leap into the undergrowth some ten yards away where it would be safe, then lost its footing and fell. The dogs were thrown into confusion during which it headed for safety but not before two dogs lay dead. The others gave chase.

"That's life," said Elizabeth stoically. "Kill or be killed. The leopard meant no harm, cubs to feed and frightened as hell. Blame the chain saw, the devil's own invention. Trees fall, scrub is flattened and the animals have nowhere to go. It will be my turn next but I have civilisation to turn to." She chuckled at the irony. "If you can call it that. I'll stay right here if you don't mind. Help me bury the dogs. I'm not as young as I was."

She wasn't the only one. I was no spring chicken myself. We dug a hole on the fringe of the clearing where the earth was soft but it was still hard work. I ached all over. We lowered the dogs into the hole and covered them over.

"Dogs will be dogs," she intoned philosophically. "If they had left the leopard alone none of this would have happened. Hungry, that's all. We all get hungry. I fed one a month ago and to show its gratitude it took one of my goats. While we're on the subject, would you care for lunch."

I politely declined. "I'd best be on my way before it gets dark. Thanks all the same. Before I leave I have something for you. If you'll excuse me." I left quickly and silently.

CHAPTER TWO

BOOKS AND THINGS

The native boys I had hired to paddle the canoe were waiting patiently. They carried the packing case between them. It is hard going in a thick jungle where even a walk of a hundred paces can have a disorientating effect if you lose concentration for a second and find you are lost, but they knew the country and didn't complain.

I wouldn't have missed the look on Elizabeth's face for the world. She watched excitedly as we emptied it; books, provisions etc. The dogs sniffed around suspiciously and the cats were ready to jump on anything that moved.

She was too overcome to express her thanks.

Tears were not far below the surface. The boys discreetly withdrew and she gave me a big kiss and then fumbled for her glasses before examining the books. I sat down, watching and waiting.

She picked the first book up that came to hand and flicked through the pages. "Where did you get this?" she enthused.

"It's Alice In Wonderland. Do you like it?"

She clapped her hands. "It's my favourite. Where did you get it?" she repeated.

"Brisbane airport. I bought the lot at knockdown price. Not my idea of a good read but there's no accounting for taste."

"Have you read it?" she asked.

I admitted I had. "Out of curiosity. In my day little

boys didn't read about little girls following white rabbits down holes. A reasonably good story though from what I remember."

She settled on a page and read it to herself before saying, "You're so kind. I couldn't have wished for a nicer present. This," she pressed a thumb on the page, "I learnt off by heart. It's the verse the White Rabbit recites to the King. I doubt if I remember it now. The memory plays tricks. I'm not young any more." She put the book down. "More tea?"

I smiled. "I can't finish what I've got. Must be the heat."

"Then have some milk," she said, and in the same breath withdrew the offer. "Sorry, I've just remembered I'm right out. I get the powdered kind. Fresh milk doesn't stay fresh long. I'd get a fridge if I could plug it in," she joked.

"You get powdered milk from the village?" I queried.

"That's right. A boy brings it with my regular order once a month."

"The goats," I pointed out, "don't they give milk?"

She laughed. "They do but it's not fit to drink. Don't ask me why. They look in fine health to me. One's pregnant. I'll wait till she's suckling and try again. Irvie liked poetry," she said suddenly. "He could commit it to memory and was word perfect. His voice was as clear as a bell. Do you like poetry?"

I shrugged. "I can take it or leave it."

"Aren't you sure? What a funny man you are."

Then she changed before my eyes. Slow co-ordination, not as it should be. Perhaps the excitement had been too much. She inched towards her seat and it took several painful minutes to sit down.

"You okay?" I said.

She put on a brave face. "Not to worry. I kid myself it's the heat but I've been in the tropics too long for that. Truth is age is catching up on me." She bore up well, her voice racked like her body but fluent and strong with a determination not to give in. "It's not every day I get visitors," she added. "If I'd known …" She took a deep breath and got some of her strength back, and then rubbed her eyes as if seeing me for the first time. "You remind me of someone, someone from the past. Your mannerisms, the way you stand. Tall, aren't you? I'm sure we've met before, yet …" She made a dismissive gesture. "Bah, don't mind me. I'm rambling again. Recapturing old memories is all I can do. Trouble is my imagination runs away with me."

I nodded. "I understand. You're a brave lady."

She corrected me. "You mean foolish lady. Who in their right mind would shut themselves off from the world with nothing but animals for company? I could die tonight and no one would know. But I'm not complaining. I chose this life. No one held a gun to my head. It's the only life I know. Travelling, settling down, moving on. An Odyssey in search of happiness, you might say. For one brief moment I thought I had found it but I was mistaken."

"Irvie?" I said.

Humour played about her lips, humour that was sad and in pain too. "Who else? The bane of my life. He walked in and bowed out after draining my life's blood. I'm not saying he did it with intent to hurt. I only wish he had gone a different way about it, that's all. No one can have that effect with design. I sometimes wonder if I had that effect on him." Her eyes met mine. "I hope not. It's enough that I suffered the agonies of hell without his suffering the same." Her eyes wavered a little. "But the pain is not so bad now. One can handle the transitory emotions but something as strong as love takes time. Even then it doesn't entirely go away. His pain is my pain, his happiness my happiness. Romantics may well ascribe it as my reason for being here and perhaps they're right, but I'm a loner by nature. Perhaps if I saw him again." She sighed wistfully.

"He might be dead and buried," I suggested.

She was firm in her belief that he wasn't. "I'll know when he is. Not a day goes by without I'm aware of his presence. It is stronger in the evening when he's relaxing."

Her brow creased in thought. "Strange, I haven't given him a thought these past couple of days. Travelling I suppose. He'll be back. It has happened before. He was very poorly a month ago, I thought I'd lost him Then he came back as clear as day. He probably has grandchildren and walks with a stick. I hope for his sake he has forgotten me, One thing, I'll never forget him."

Her glasses fell off and she fumbled for them. I picked them up and returned them to her.

"Thank you. I'll let you into a little secret," she confided. "I'm as blind as a bat without them. Even with them I still need a magnifying glass when reading."

"The verse," I pointed out, "you read that."

She chuckled mischievously. "Perhaps my memory isn't so bad after all. I didn't even know what book it was until you told me. A joke. Hope you don't mind."

"I don't mind."

She screwed up her eyes and examined me closely.

"Tall, aren't you?"

I didn't say anything.

"Name?"

"Yes, I have a name."

She went drowsy, her head fell forward and in no

time she was asleep. A cat jumped on her lap and the dogs came to her side. They knew I meant no harm but were taking no chances. Then as suddenly she was awake.

"Don't mind me," she said. "I have my good days and bad days. If you feel sorry for me – Don't. Where my eyesight leaves off instinct takes over. I can see outline, then there's the dogs. They're my eyes." She took a deep breath. "Not much of a hostess, am I? Nodding off is getting to be a habit. I should see a doctor but who would take care of my family? The village is a five-day round trip and they might not let me come back." She couldn't have been more emphatic. "I'll stay right here if you don't mind. No amount of medicine can compensate for the happiness I have here." She embraced each dog in turn and the cats purred contentedly. One dog got jealous and bared its teeth.

"That's Fang," she said. "He's number one now Spike and Figgy have gone. A good dog to have around but unpredictable. Spike kept him in line. Spike was the fighter. That's why he was killed. No dog is a match for a leopard but Spike wouldn't have it any other way. Figgy just happened to be there. He was the cautious one but was killed all the same. Two down, three to go."

The others rallied around obediently as if understanding every word she said. I glanced outside. The sky was overcast and there was pressure in the air. I prepared to leave. "Something tells me I had better be off before a storm brews up," I said. "Anyone you want to be remembered to? Friend, cousin maybe?"

Her reply came as no surprise. "You are very kind but I've no one. My cousin died five years ago."

"Irvie? I could look him up if he's alive," I suggested.

"He's alive," she assured me, "as sure as you're standing there. More alive than he ever was and so close

I feel I can almost touch him. As for looking him up! Whatever for, to dig over old bones? I prefer to leave things as they are and remember him as he was. Those eyes and that voice, that's what I want to take to the grave." She turned her back to me and scribbled something and then faced me again. "Here, take it, this is for you." She pressed a diary into my hand. "Don't read it until you're far away from here, promise."

"Promise."

At the first drop of rain we said goodbye. She accompanied me to the edge of the clearing, holding my hand.

"Don't think me bitter in my old age," she said. "I've had my moments, I'm not complaining. It has been a pleasure meeting you. Hope your journey hasn't been wasted." Her eyes moistened. "Pity you have to leave so soon but everything comes to an end." She took my hand. "Thank you. Take care."

I kissed her lightly on the cheek. "I will," walked away and didn't look back.

CHAPTER THREE

THE DIARY

When I got back to the canoe dusk was falling. Chattering monkeys sent us on our way. The boys took it in turn to paddle, their glances telling me I had come all this way for nothing. But I knew different. I had found out all I wanted to know.

The river swirled and chopped and overhanging branches made progress difficult. One false move and the canoe would capsize and it would be all over. But the boys knew what they were doing. I cursed myself for not starting out earlier but every moment with Elizabeth was precious. I felt a great sense of achievement fringed with sadness yet didn't feel sad. Relieved if anything that she had the courage to carry on.

I turned my attention to the river. No telling what lurked beneath the surface, and the fact that the rainforest seemed to be closing in on us didn't help my claustrophobia any, or having to cling on for dear life against the swaying motion of the canoe. The boys were used to it.

On reflection, perhaps looking up Elizabeth wasn't such a good idea. Opening old wounds was the last thing I wanted to do. It could be argued that I should have minded my own business and left her alone with her memories, that nothing had come of it but I knew different. I smiled and hoped she was smiling too. I took out the diary and in the fading light could just make out the name Elizabeth in gold relief on the cover. The pages were blurred. I put the diary away.

*****

We followed down the river to a vast tract of grassland from where we travelled on foot. Any other time we could have taken the canoe to the edge of Newtown where the river empties into the sea, but the plains had flooded and to go any further would be a risk not worth taking.

The boys tied the canoe to a tree that was rotting away with the result that the canoe slipped its moorings damaging its side and drifted downstream. It was then I discovered my watch was missing. It had fallen from my wrist and was in the bottom of the canoe, and there was nothing I could do. Taking a leaf out of Elizabeth's book, I shrugged it off as one of those things.

We kept a lookout for leopards, alligators, buffalo and feral bulls, descendants of a herd of Herefords brought over by settlers who didn't settle for long when they learned there was no demand for English beef. Bulls and buffalo are a major threat on the island apart from the chain saw. When not grazing they go looking for trouble, leopards are cunning and always on the move while alligators; well, alligators are alligators. There are plenty of wild boar so nobody goes hungry; and monkeys if they are foolish enough to get caught, not forgetting the odd lizard for a quick snack. Leopards handle population control on land and alligators keep the river tidy, a perfect arrangement all around. Occasionally an alligator makes a sortie on land and a bull drives him back.

*****

It was coming up to midnight when we got back to the village, pretentiously called Newtown because it's not new and not a town. The Commissionaire's house, half a dozen cabins and a tarpaulin draped over wooden uprights made it look like a deserted outpost.

I was to get the boat to Brisbane the next morning and then a flight home. Part of me wanted to go and part of me wanted to stay. My heart thumped as I said goodbye to the boys and made my way to my cabin. Without them I was vulnerable. Fading snatches of conversation and laughter as they disappeared into the gloom increased my vulnerability. I had two hundred yards to go.

*****

I disturbed a bush pig that came from behind a thicket and caught me a glancing blow on the thigh before disappearing into the night. I was congratulating myself on my good fortune when it came back to finish me off when a leopard came to my rescue. There was a scuffle, a few grunts and it was all over. A leopard turns the legs to jelly from any distance, never mind when you can reach out and touch it. Its eyes were luminous and glowing with hate as it looked at me. And when it hissed and arched its back I thought my time had come. Fortunately, it had made a kill and was satisfied. My thigh started to throb. It wasn't broken because I could still walk but it hurt all the same. The leopard dragged the bush pig out of sight and I heaved a sigh of relief.

I thought I saw pinpricks of light through the trees. Imagination probably. If I took my time I should be all right. While not lost exactly, I wasn't altogether sure I was going the right way. My thigh started up again and I was forced to rest. Calling for help was out of the question, it might bring the leopard back. I reflected on what Elizabeth would do in my position. Charmed the leopard, probably, into escorting her home. And that was where we were different. She could make decisions, pick up where she left off and try again. I was apt to dither, and by the time I had made up my mind it was too late. She was strong, I wasn't.

*****

I struggled to my feet and balanced on one leg. It took me ages to find a branch suitable enough to serve as a crutch and twice as long to hack it into shape. A snake fell from above and landed on my shoulder, and before I could cry out it slithered away into the undergrowth. I didn't know who was the more startled, that or me. I resumed my journey, moving as I fast as I could. My thigh stopped hurting and went numb. It was more serious than I thought.

Shadows moved around me, silent, furtive.

I went dizzy and had visions of glaring colours almost blinding me. The shadows disappeared. The isolation was closing in on me. I tried not to panic and rubbed the circulation back into my leg. I ached all over. I hobbled as best I could and must have cut a pathetic figure.

The moon through the trees waxed and waned. The strain was taking its toll and I had to rest again. A wild cat passed with a rat in its mouth. The rat writhed and squealed pathetically knowing it was doomed. I lay back exhausted and closed my eyes. Elizabeth came to me and the words, "One can handle the transitory emotions people have but something as strong as love takes time. His pain is my pain, his happiness my happiness," echoed in my mind. It had a certain poignancy, a lucidity of having won and lost. But she wasn't bitter. She bore no grudge, taking life as it comes, comforted by her memories, crying when no one was there. She wasn't alone. Others were crying too.

*****

A light shone in the Commissionaire's office and a typewriter tapped away. I went directly to my cabin. Heaven knows how I made it; a cast-iron will to survive, I suppose. Perhaps Elizabeth's resolve not to give in had rubbed off on me. I certainly felt difference. Even my leg came back to life.

I was tired but sleep was out of the question. I had too much on my mind. Elizabeth was probably asleep by now or quoting from Alice, tucked up in her hammock watched over by her dogs. Fang would take care of her. If he didn't, the others would. They were her family. Her only enemy was the chain saw. Was a reclusive life in the rainforest what she really wanted? Only she can answer that. In my mind I rolled back the years. Flashing eyes and bursts of laughter were things of the past but the smile was still there.

I lit the oil lamp and took a photograph from my wallet of how I remembered her. Auburn hair, pouting lips, twinkling eyes. Even in the photograph her individuality shone through, an awareness that she was different, world-wise without being blasé, travel-weary yet fresh, an eagerness to be accepted that would never be. Or was it she had found what she was looking for - A patch in the rainforest she called home but would never be a real home without Irvie? Though he was never far away.

In a funny way I felt she was with me. I was restless, and paced up and down trying to get my thoughts together. I took a shower, a contraption of bamboo, rope and an outside water butt, after which I nibbled a sandwich and sipped warm tea. I wasn't feeling too good. Why I had taken it upon myself to travel halfway round the world raised questions regarding my sanity, but I knew what I was doing and no amount of explaining would convince others that it had been worthwhile. 'Leave well alone' they say. "No good will come of it.' Little they knew of the urge to see her just one more time had nagged me for more than I care to remember.

My hands were shaking as I opened the diary. It hadn't been lying idle. Although the pages were dogeared, the script was bright and clear as if it had been written that morning. On closer inspection I noticed fresh ink traced the original text, some passages clearer than others. Elizabeth's contributions were the more faded, the others madrigals of high intensity, declarations of love.

I sat down. The hours passed. The flickering lamp and nocturnal sounds of the rainforest didn't disturb me. As I read on memories came flooding back to me, and I could hear Elizabeth's pounding heart and see her smiling face as she pulled up tufts of heather and threw them at me and then run away pretending to stumble to make me think I was faster than she was when all the time I knew what she was doing. I reflected on many things, not least the life she chose. Whatever its whys and wherefores, the life of a recluse wasn't for me. But who knows? I turned to the last page. Scrawled across the text in bold capitals was the message: 'Irvie, you're late. I've been expecting you. Now I can rest in peace. Give my love to little Kieron.'

The lamp dimmed and went out. I struck a match but the wick was damp or something and didn't come up so bright. A spring of heather was pressed into the diary. I flicked through the pages and staring me in the face was what I remembered the most: 'I fell for your charms …And my arms held you tight.' The diary slipped from my fingers. I got a headache. Elizabeth made contact of some kind. It came through loud and clear. The headache went away and the lamp came up bright again. I steadied myself, sat down and murmured, "Elizabeth is dying." In the final moments I lived in her mind, and then she closed her eyes for the last time. In a vague kind of way we were running over the heather, her teasing, me trying to catch up. Then she slipped from my grasp. Footsteps sounded outside. Someone rapped the door.

It was the Commissionaire. "Why didn't you tell me you were back, Mr Irvine? You're too old for this sort of thing. How is the old girl?"

CHAPTER FOUR

TWENTY YEARS LATER

I'm little Kieron, only I'm grown up now; six-foot four, eighteen-stone, thirty-five years old and as fit as a fiddle. Elizabeth's and Irvie's diaries are on the bookshelf by my side. I've read them so many times I can quote them word for word.

I was brought up in a children's home and always wondered who my parents were until a stranger knocked on my door one Sunday afternoon. Tall, pale and unsteady on his feet, I put him in his mid-seventies. He introduced himself as Stewart Irvine and claimed to be my father. If I showed no emotion it was because I was a little startled and didn't altogether believe him, although we did share the same surname.

Suspicious, I invited him inside. He told me he had traced me through Missing Persons, and his reason for visiting me was he didn't have long to live and wanted to tell me before he died how he and Elizabeth, my mother, had met, the happy times they had together, Elizabeth going on her travels and their final meeting on the South Sea Island of Pago Mara where she died.

He gave me the diaries. "These are yours," he said. "Elizabeth is buried where she died. Her possessions remain untouched as she would have wished. She had a good Christian burial. All her friends were there. If you visit her grave put a bunch of flowers on for me, will you?"

Not once did he refer to Elizabeth as my mother. Perhaps, after so many years, he was embarrassed and felt guilty at having not visited me before. I would call her Elizabeth too. Not out of disrespect but because I considered it presumptuous, if not improper, until I got used to the idea. After all, it's not every day you discover you have a mother and a father.

No sooner had he finished talking than he shook my hand and left, no tears, no recriminations. I never saw him again. He died two months later leaving me twenty thousand pounds. Not that I'm complaining but felt lousy about taking it, and lousier still when I found out I was his only son and heir. I didn't feel like a son and heir. I didn't even feel like a son. I hardly knew him.

But this was soon remedied, however, when I read the diaries, after which it was as if I had known him and Elizabeth all my life. The intensity of their love for each other leapt out of every page, and the circumstances in which they parted inevitable otherwise it wouldn't have lasted so long. Distance lends enchantment, they say. The fact that he was married but not to Elizabeth rankled a little, but no matter. It was all over now.

Where Elizabeth's diary was an elegy for time passed and lost love, Irvie's was a masterpiece of objective, purpose and prose, occasionally drifting into spasms of regret where one felt he couldn't help himself. A map of Pago Mara, ringed in pencil on a map of the New Hebrides in the South Pacific, was coloured green for rainforest, brown for mountains, blue for rivers and yellow for valleys. The letter E marked the spot where Elizabeth was buried, plus other symbols with index denoting other landmarks. Dozens of smaller islands surrounded it like a string of beads. Great pains had been taken to show me where to go. Not only that, Irvie had given me a family history, something to look back on, something more than just a name. If only for that I would visit Elizabeth's grave. But first I must find out how to get there.

*****

I lived in a flat on the edge of town, a three-room affair, with a three-piece suite, couple of chairs, table, sideboard and a telephone on a wrought iron stand. Also there was a TV, CD and letters and magazines in a letter rack. On the walls were scenes of the Scottish Highlands and wide-open spaces. I was a lecturer on natural history, loved camping holidays, amateur boxing and did regular work-outs at the local gym.

*****

Heidi was my sweetheart, blonde, pretty, going in and out at the right places, who could be an angel or the very devil when the mood took her. She lived next door. I was nodding off on the settee when she charged into the room like a herd of elephants.

I wasn't in the best of moods. I sat up and rubbed my eyes. "Can't you make less noise?"

She pulled a face. "The door was open. Anyone could walk in."

I yawned. "They did. What time is it?"

"Nine-thirty Monday morning. You were late for work and I let you sleep in. I'm having a day off too."

"It's the end of term," I reminded her, "or have you forgotten? I don't go back for another six weeks. What have you to tell me?"

She sat beside me. "What makes you think I've something to tell you?"

"Because you're not usually so cheerful this time in the morning."

"I'm cheerful when it suits me," she replied.

"So you are. Well, I'm waiting."

She frowned. "Waiting for what?"

"What you're bursting at the seams to tell me."

She looked at me steadily. "Not good news, I'm afraid."

I yawned again. "It never is. I'm still recovering from the last news I heard."

She perked up. "Why, what was it?"

"Nothing you would understand."

"Aren't you going to tell me?"

"No, you tell me."

"Two men called this morning," she began. "I told them you were out of town."

"Where did you see them?" I asked.

"They were about to ring your doorbell. I live next door, remember."

I grunted. "What did they want?"

"Your car. You're six months behind with the payments."

I raised my voice. "They tell you that?"

She nodded. "Thy don't stand on ceremony. If they did they'd be out of business. I'll lend you the money if you haven't got it."

I squeezed her hand. "You're an angel but no thanks. Two months ago I'd have snatched your hand off. Lady Luck has smiled on me since then." I didn't tell her about Irvine and my inheritance. She wouldn't understand.

She was delighted. "You've won the lottery."

"Not exactly.

Delight turned to disappointment. "You haven't won the lottery."

I told her again she wouldn't understand, stood up and made for the kitchen. "Tea or coffee?" I said.

She stood in my way. "Kiss me."

I kissed her.

She pouted her lips. "Kiss me again."

It wasn't a kiss she wanted but an argument. I pushed past her and finished what I set out to do and brought in two coffees. For no reason she slapped my face. But that was her. She didn't need a reason. She just went ahead and did it.

I warned her not to do it again.

She laughed in my face. "I'll do whatever I like."

I restrained myself and put the coffees down. "Why don't you grow up?"

She clamped her teeth over her bottom lip and almost bit off. "And why don't you drop dead?"

I took it with my usual tolerance. Humouring her was the only thing I could do but one day she would go too far. Still, we were lovers and true love never runs smooth. Whether we were actually in love is another matter. I might have been in love with her. She certainly wasn't in love with me.

It was some time before she spoke. "Where are you taking me tonight?" She wanted to say sorry but didn't know how to.

"We don't go out Mondays," I told her.

She worried her bottom lip again. "There's no law against going out Mondays. There's a new place opened on Thurland Street – Frankie's Bar. It's only been in business a week and people are queuing to get in already."

"Not exactly the sort place for a college lecturer," I murmured and then added, "What do you say to the South Seas?"

She frowned. "What about the South Seas?"

"Would you like to go to the South Seas, a South Sea Island?"

"Sleepy lagoon and tropical moon?" she spat sarcastically.

"Take it or leave it."

"You mean you're serious?"

"Never been more so. Sun-soaked beaches, swaying palms."

"Frankie's Bar," she repeated, "and don't argue."

"It won't cost you a penny."

She chewed on it. "What will we use for money?"

"I've been saving for a rainy day."

Her eyes lit up. "How much?"

"That's for me to know and not for you to ask."

She went cute and helpless and looked at me out of the tops of her eyes. "You wouldn't be having little tiddykins on, now would you? I mean, you did say the South Seas?" Her voice was as sultry as she could make it.

"You heard me."

"Tiddykins wouldn't like it if you were pulling her leg."

"Now why would I do that?"

"You are telling the truth?"

I put a hand on my heart. "Scout's honour."

She came up close and looked dreamily into my eyes. "Why didn't you say so?"

Her perfume was choking me. "I did."

She pulled me back on the settee. "When do we start packing."

*****

Acquiring travel brochures from a travel agency, I got passports and other documents, and, making sure

Irvie's map was safely tucked away, we were off. We flew to Brisbane and stayed the night in the airport hotel. It was the first time Heidi had been in a hotel and I wouldn't have missed the look on her face for the world. I bought her a gold locket and we dined off the finest silver. It was the holiday of a lifetime and she was on her best behaviour.

*****

The next morning I hired a yacht for the final leg of the journey and told the captain my reason for going there. He was sympathetic but not pleased.

"Pago Mara, hey? I don't like the idea of putting you off there," he declared. "A logging company set up business there years ago and pulled out on account of reefs and its high, rocky coastline. It used to be navigable when longboats were the fashion but not any more. Maybe it's your modern vessels with deeper drafts or poor navigation skills, your guess is as good as mine. More likely it's just that the island isn't worth visiting and nobody knows the waters any more. There is a way through if you know whet you're doing. If not," he put his thumbs down, "you go to the bottom. Shipping trees proved costlier than cutting them down. Pity all rainforests aren't surrounded by reefs and cliffs. When the logging company left the natives went with them, including a Commissionaire from bygone days who was past his sell by date. Plans to build coffee plantations and orange groves were forgotten. There are a few good spots," he added, "sandy beaches, lagoons, that sort of thing if you know where to look."

I wasn't put off. I told him if he picked us up two weeks later I would make it worth his while.

"I didn't say I was taking you there yet," he growled.

I repeated my offer.

He grunted, "Okay, but don't say I didn't warn you."

I elicited a promise to keep it to himself. The last thing I wanted was for Heidi to find out. As far as she was concerned it was just a holiday, pure and simple, and I didn't want to spoil her fun. If she knew the truth I wouldn't hear the last of it. I would keep it from her if it killed me.

*****

Heidi lived up to expectations and flirted with the crew to such an extent that the captain warned her that if she didn't behave he would turn back and cancel the trip.

From then on she behaved herself and joined me as we both gazed at the vast blue ocean by day and marvelled at the star-studded sky by night. On the fifth day the sky clouded over and there was pressure in the air. Heidi retired to the cabin. Despite the captain's advice, I stayed on deck and watched the storm come up from the horizon, tumbling towards us like a battering ram crushing everything in its path. Then as suddenly as it started it stopped, the ocean calm and untroubled as before.

*****

On the third day Pago Mara came into view. Heidi stood transfixed, saying it was what she had always dreamed of. Although it was what I wanted to hear her say, I was too blasé to be impressed by sleepy lagoons and sun-drenched beaches, even if what the captain said was true.

"You're lucky," he said, "the tide's out, you can see the beach. It's one of the few beaches that are safe to land but you can never be sure. Them reefs are everywhere. We'll put you ashore in a dinghy. Flat-bottomed see. It skims right over them. See you in two weeks, Good luck."

They lowered a dinghy with a hamper of provisions and saw us on our way. Two of the crew took us ashore. The beach was golden brown, I had never seen so much sand. We watched the dinghy make the return journey, and the yacht disappear over the horizon.

CHAPTER FIVE

THE STRANGER

We walked together holding hands, awe-stricken by the giant fern that swayed in the sea breeze, and plants the like of which we had never seen before. We found a deserted cabin a little way into the interior that offered nothing in the way of creature comforts but would keep out the mosquitoes. It was cluttered with beds, lockers and all the paraphernalia of having once been lived in.

On our first night we got off to a bad start. Heidi went into a sulk, refusing to talk. I thought at first she had overheard me talking to the captain and didn't like my going behind her back, but I was wrong so put it down to disappointment. What she had dreamed of had turned sour. Sun-drenched beaches and swaying palms aren't all they're cracked up to be.

The first morning we had egg, bacon and a pot of tea for breakfast, getting water from the river and not forgetting to boil it. There was game, of course, to vary our diet, fish and plenty of fruit. Not that Heidi was the least bit interested. Her silence developed into a brooding reticence that precluded all contact with me. She didn't reply when I asked what was wrong.

*****

On the second day we had a visitor, a man in his thirties, tall, athletic, as broad as an ox. He was shy at first but didn't need a lot of persuading to make himself at home. Out of politeness I poured him a mug of coffee.

In no time he was the life and soul of the party and gave us a tune on his mouth organ. The change in Heidi was amazing. She was her old self again, alive, talkative, a smile on her face. Even more amazing was she sat beside him as if I wasn't there. I controlled my anger. He introduced himself as Danny but didn't say where he was from or what he was doing there.

Anger turned to jealousy when she hung on to his every word, and, if that wasn't enough winked at him when she thought I wasn't looking. Not wanting to make a scene, I passed it off as an eagerness to please, her way of making him feel at home. But I kept my eye on them all the same.

They spent a lot of time together during the next two days, then on the third day he disappeared, No thanks, by your leave, kiss my backside, nothing; he just upped and went. That's gratitude for you, but I can't say I wasn't pleased to see the back of him. Heidi went back into her shell and we were back where we started.

*****

Tuesday into the second week she disappeared too. I searched the scrub surrounding the cabin calling her name and in the silence thought I heard laughter. I searched far and wide and then headed for the beach thinking perhaps she had gone for a swim. In her state of mind she was liable to do anything. It occurred to me that it wasn't outside the bounds of possibility that she and Danny had arranged a rendezvous so they could be together, but suspicion is not proof. I scoured the beach and made my way back to the cabin.

Chattering monkeys accompanied me on my way, the birds kept their distance and shadows in the trees sharpened my perception. Enchanted by the sights, sounds and scents now I was on my own, I was as bewildered as any stranger might be. It was hard going; ankle-breaking roots, clinging vine and sprawling bushes hampered my every step. The leaf mould alone contained hundreds of insects I had never seen before, while other wildlife of every shape and form thrived under rotting logs, in hollow trees, and below and above the canopy from monkeys and fruit bats to birds of prey and birds so exquisitely coloured as to defy description and imagination. But don't go on appearances. Pretty birds can be pretty brutal sometimes, like the one I saw bashing an insect to death on a branch and another killing a beetle twice its size before eating it.

*****

After a couple of hours I rested. New sounds, muffled, furtive, obtruded themselves above the rest. At first I didn't realise they were different, then, if I wasn't mistaken, they were human footfalls. My pulse raced. I called Heidi's name. No response, then I felt dozens of eyes upon me. The monkeys stopped chattering and the birds flew away, then it was silent.

Of course, I had no more proof that the footfalls were human any more than I could prove I was being watched. The trees rustled and the eyes went away. Then I thought I saw a bulging forehead and dark, brooding eyes poking from behind a copse of wild orchids. I investigated. Nothing. The powdery soil bore no trace of footprints human or otherwise, and then out of the silence came a chorus of wails so melancholy my heart missed a beat. I threshed through the trees in the direction they came from. Monkeys glided through the branches like ghosts and life form stirred beneath my feet. Then, as soon as the wails started they stopped, followed by rasping coughs not unlike the bark of a dog. A turkey cock passed by with its brood watched by a fallow deer from a distance that was suddenly dragged into the undergrowth. A deep-throated roar preceded a pitiful squeal as a leopard dragging it by its throat came into view. The turkey cock ushered its brood away as quickly as possible and I followed.

*****

As I approached the cabin music trickled to my ears. I crept up to the window and saw Danny stretched out on a bed, eyes closed, radio blaring. I ducked down when I heard someone coming. It was Heidi in the bikini she had packed in the trunk and which I thought she would never wear. She passed within inches of me and I suppressed an urge to jump out and put my hands round her throat. But the truth is all fight had been knocked out of me. Even so I couldn't take my eyes off her. She glided rather than walked.

I had never seen her looking so lovely.

In my clumsiness I trod on a twig and it cracked like a pistol shot, She shot off through the trees. I was getting used to the rainforest by now and, although she had a head start, I had no trouble keeping up with her. Catching her was another matter. She was fitter than I gave her credit for. I was whipped by branches and hampered by vines whereas her progress was smooth and unimpeded. She crossed a grass clearing heading for the beach. Her hair, blown by the wind coupled with her near-nakedness bestowed on her the vigour and beauty of an Amazon. It was hard to believe she was the same woman I met in the local park two years previously. If only we could talk. But

43

I had to catch her first and I couldn't see that happening unless she broke both legs.

*****

By the time I reached the clearing she had disappeared. Guttural coughs rose above the other sounds that grew to rasping screams. A single cry, unmistakably human, came from the same direction. I ran forward with no thought for myself, and in my haste fell through a wall of hibiscus and found myself in an amphitheatre walled in on three sides by terraces built with enormous blocks of stone.

On the ground was a baboon - usually found in Africa and Asia but scattered around the South Pacific and similar climes; ugly and ferocious with hind and fore limbs roughly the same size, enabling it to walk on all fours. Adorned in a fantastic array of colours, the males twice the size of females, this one had a red and blue face and sleek brown body, and stood around 1.10 metres. Its jaw was remarkably strong with tusks capable of inflicting a very severe wound. Seldom seen in forests, they make their home among the rocks, though can take to the trees when necessary.

It mocked and jeered its fellows, who responded with hisses and barks from the ledges above. When they saw me they stopped. Those on the ledges urged the one on the ground to do something. It didn't let them down and approached me on all fours, barking, showing its teeth. Unimpressed, I looked around for Heidi, too preoccupied to lend myself to some foolish primitive ritual I wanted no part of. Fear was the last of my emotions. It wasn't sure what to do. I knew exactly what I was going to do. I was in a hurry and it was in my way.

I advanced a step and it backed off, its uncertainty increasing in proportion to its bewilderment. The others stamped their feet and struck up a chorus of frenzied shrieks of impatience to get it over with. Without warning it leapt for my throat but I was ready. I stepped to one side at the same time bringing my fist across catching it on the jaw. It shrieked as it sailed over my shoulder twisting and turning before it hit the ground. I was on it before it had time to could recover, picked it up and threw it as far as I could. It hit the ground again, rolled over and lay still. Cries and shrieks subsided to howls of dismay.

Then a young male, eager to prove himself, jumped from a ledge to take up the challenge and just as eagerly I turned and walked away. As I said, fear didn't enter into it. I was determined to find Heidi and nothing else mattered. The baboon had taken me on and paid the price, and the next in line wasn't going to inherit the role of leader at my expense.

CHAPTER SIX

LIES AND EXCUSES

I was about to give up all hope of finding Heidi when she found me. I stopped at a fork in the path deciding which way to go when she came from the opposite direction and decided for me. I grabbed hold of her before she could get away. She struggled at first and when she realised she couldn't break free she snuggled up close.

"I thought you were ..." she started to say and changed her mind "Oh, never mind, I owe you an explanation. We can't talk here. Come, I'll show you. It's where I hid from those horrible monkeys. A leopard took one of their young and they tried to take it out on me." She took my hand and I followed.

*****

It was a bleak and brooding milieu where trees poke skeletal fingers at the sky. Cracks in a carpet of floating moss bore testimony to the countless unsuspecting animals that had stepped in and were sucked out of sight: A mire; a quivering mass of rotting vegetation; a graveyard shunned by everybody except the unwary. Not the best place to settle our differences but we needed to talk. I'd have words with Danny later.

When I asked why she had run away, she said she thought I was Danny, which struck me as odd since she must have known he was in the cabin. The answers to my next questions didn't make sense either, so I told her what was on my mind, reminding her that she had flirted with Danny with no thought for my feelings, pretended to go missing and doubled back to be alone with him when she thought I was miles away, and changed into the bikini for his benefit. In my anger I clenched my fists and she shrank back when the last thing I wanted to do was frighten her.

We sat down. I told her about the baboons. She wasn't interested. I commented on the weather. She wasn't interested in that either. And it was then I knew we could never start again and pick up where we left off unless she changed her ways and convinced me there was nothing between her and Danny. Even so, I couldn't see how things could ever be the same again. It wasn't just the flirting. It was the way they looked at each other.

"I don't deny I was infatuated with him when he first arrived," she cried. "I thought he was different and had a crazy idea he could give me what I wanted when all the time I wanted you, only I didn't realise it at the time. When he disappeared I went looking for him. He was no longer the Prince Charming I thought he was, more wolf in sheep's clothing. He jumped on me like a wild animal. I thought the heat had got to him and he didn't know what he was doing, but he knew what he was doing all right. I struggled but he was too strong. He took me to the cabin. I prayed you would turn up but you didn't. I put the bikini on because he tore my dress and I couldn't find anything else to wear."

She brought a sexual frisson in the guise of being conscious of the skimpy way she was dressed and fooled no one, least of all me. She might be telling the truth, of course, but I was far from satisfied. "What happened when you got to the cabin?" I asked.

Tears were not far below the surface. "What do you think?"

It was all I could to control my anger. "You mean..?" I didn't finish.

Her voice trembled. "Do I have to go into detail? I said he was too strong for me. There was nothing I could do."

"How did you get away?" I asked.

"He fell asleep and I saw my chance," she replied. "It was the heat, after all. I left the cabin and was deciding which way to go when I heard a twig snap and took off as fast as my legs could carry me. If I had known it was you …"

I still wasn't satisfied. "You don't look as if you've been mauled," I said. "True or false, I'll maul him when I get my hands on him."

She burst into tears and didn't say another word.

It wasn't the moody silence as before, more a plea to forgive and forget without actually saying so. My suspicion grew. If what I was thinking was true she certainly had nerve, deliberately sending me on a wild goose chase at the risk of being eaten alive, and now she wanted us to be as we were as if nothing had happened. As much as I loved her I couldn't find it in my heart to forgive and forget. Perhaps I had judged her too harshly. Perhaps. We'd see.

The moss moved and bubbles rose to the top as something surfaced. A tiny lizard emerged from the murky depths, scrambled up the side and melted into the undergrowth. Heidi's revulsion made her to snuggle up to me again. The mire, a graveyard for many, provided a living for a few.

*****

Finding our way back to the cabin was easy. It found us. Danny was nowhere to be seen.

I turned to her. "Okay, you've had your little joke, where is he? I know he's around. If this is another one of your tricks …"

"No trick, honest," she assured me. "You don't believe a word I say. I don't know where he is any more than you do. You've got to believe me."

She was right. I didn't believe a word she said. "Where is he?" I repeated.

More tears. "He must have woken up when he heard us coming."

I scoffed. "Any excuse is better than none."

"But …"

I stopped her. "Save it."

In the distance came grunts and wails. She froze. Her eyes searched mine. If she had known what I was thinking she'd be off once more and I might never see her again. No point in making her more nervous than she was. Anyway, it might mean nothing. Noises are heard in the rainforest all the time. I passed it off. Provided she didn't come to any harm; and she wouldn't - I'd see to that. I was okay. I could take care of myself.

"We'll look for him together," I said. "He can't be far away. I'll tell you what I think when I hear what he's got to say. I can't wait to get you two together."

"How many times do I have to tell you?" she cried. "He forced himself on me. You don't believe me no matter what I say. He's probably miles away by now."

"Not if he has any sense," I said.

"What do you mean?"

"He doesn't know the rainforest as well as I do."

Before I knew what I was doing I took her in my arms. Don't ask me why except she was my sweetheart and for that reason, in spite of my better judgement, I was prepared to give her the benefit of the doubt. Perhaps I had blown up a harmless flirtation out of proportion and read something that wasn't there. Perhaps I was jealous. I had a right to be jealous. Heidi was a beautiful woman.

Whether she meant to or not, she put a hand on mine and whispered, "You're a good man."

I didn't know about that. All I knew was I was doing what I thought was right. Guilty or innocent, I wasn't sure. It wasn't that I flattered Danny for thinking she regarded him as any more than a novelty as much as I considered her sharp enough to see him for what he was. Bulging muscles and a crinkly smile may attract the girls but don't keep them. I had the muscle but not the smile.

I looked around. It was strangely silent. The trees and undergrowth were devoid of life. Close by came coughs and barks.

"What is it?" she said.

I lowered my voice. "Not another word."

*****

A face designed by the devil and fringed with whiskers poked from behind a bush. It was a leopard. On my own I would have made as much noise as I could and driven it away but I had Heidi to think of. It might panic and do anything, a risk I wasn't prepared to take. There was only thing for it; put Heidi somewhere safe. She protested when I urged her to follow me. I took her to the safety of a hideaway between two rocks and told her to stay there.

I had barely got her settled when a scream broke the silence. I ran back to the cabin. Danny had returned and the leopard had him by the throat. I leapt on the leopard's back, all eighteen-stone of me, pinning it down, put my hands round its throat and squeezed. It put up the fight of its life before giving a final shudder and lay still. But it was too late. Danny's throat was ripped out. A swelling between the leopard's eyes bore testimony to the fight he had put up but fists are no match for fangs. Sneaking up from behind it, I went through his pockets. No identification, nothing. I picked up the mouth organ and blew a few notes.

Outside, the eyes I felt earlier watched me from the bushes. No grunts, barks. They had chased the leopard into the cabin and I had done their dirty work for them. But I didn't mind. It could have been worse. I could have gone the same way as Danny.

I set off briskly, retracing my steps, looking forward to spending the remainder of the holiday with Heidi.

I wouldn't let her know what had happened unless I had to.

She wouldn't believe me anyway. Thinking about it, it was a shame Danny had to go that way but it wasn't my doing. I tried to save him.

*****

Reaching the hollow, I put the mouth organ to my lips and blew a tune of sorts. The response was startling. Heidi appeared blinded by tears and buried her face in my chest, laughing and crying at the same time. Even before she spoke I knew I had been fooling no one but myself and my suspicions had been right all along.

"Danny, thank God you're safe. I didn't think I'd ever see you again."

And she wouldn't but I didn't have the heart to say

so. "You've still got me," I murmured.

She was shocked at hearing my voice and her eyes, met mine; her silence more eloquent than words. It seemed as if we were alone but I knew different.

I dug a grave for Danny in the bushes where it wouldn't be seen and showed her the dead leopard, telling her what had happened in case she thought I had killed him in a jealous rage. It wasn't to show how tough I was. I had nothing to prove. I did what I had to and would have done the same for anyone. Leopards have to eat, I guess, but not when I'm around.

She showed no emotion as I shovelled the last bit of earth on Danny's grave. It was a brief ceremony after which I fashioned a cross out of twigs and said a little prayer. Everyone's entitled to a decent burial, even Danny.

They were still watching but I didn't let on. They wouldn't bother us because I had got rid of the leopard but held on to the shovel all the same. Heidi saw their inquisitive faces and screamed as they shuffled away in twos and threes. I hoped that was the last I would see of them. Belligerent by nature, they appeared, nonetheless, to accept me but one can't be too careful.

*****

Two days to go before the yacht was due. Two long days of misery and tears but not if I could help it. You can't bring back the dead.

Cheering her up was out of the question. She wouldn't even talk. All she wanted to do was to be left alone.

Indeed, it was questionable if she knew I was there. I took it philosophically, simply because I could do nothing else. Shouting at her wouldn't help.

I must have dozed off because the next thing I knew she was disappearing through the trees. I was after her like a shot. She was headed for the mire where we talked. Her stride wasn't the uncertain stumbling of panic but the smooth acceleration of someone who knows where they're going. Not once did she look back but she knew I was there.

*****

It was still bleak and brooding, the same skeletal fingers poked towards the sky and the mass of rotting vegetation still beckoned the unwary. What was different was a roebuck had stumbled in, struggled to get free and died from exhaustion with its antlers caught in a thicket. There was no sign of Heidi. I searched the undergrowth and found the gold locket I had bought her. The clasp had broken and it had fallen from her neck. It was hard to believe she had suffered the same fate as the roebuck. Panic-stricken, she didn't look where she was going. The roebuck almost made it. Heidi didn't stand a chance. I made my way back to the cabin.

CHAPTER SEVEN

THE FINAL GOODBYE

I awoke the next morning with a start. There was a commotion outside. A fawn had wandered up exhausted with a pack of wild dogs snapping at its heels. I threw water on them and the stubborn ones I waded into with a spade. Three lay dead. Even then they didn't give up. While some distracted me, others pulled the fawn down and it was then I lost my temper. I waded into them again, punching and kicking, accounting for three more. The others turned and ran away. The fawn looked at me with the saddest eyes I have seen. One leg was chewed to the bone and it was squealing pitifully. I raised the shovel above my head and brought it down as hard as I could. There was nothing else I could do. I threw the dogs in a heap, set fire to them and buried the fawn.

I spent the rest of the day pottering around, killing time until the next morning when the yacht was scheduled to arrive. As the day wore on I felt better but would never be the same. I was not only the recipient of the transient emotions one ponders for a moment and forgets, but the primordial instinct to survive, kill or be killed, run until you can run no more.

*****

Above the usual sounds rose the occasional cough. I had an urge to return to the mire. It was a million to one chance that Heidi was alive and a chance worth taking, so I set off with the shovel feeling like the last man on earth. I lost my way. Don't ask me how except I wasn't myself. I must have walked miles because the next thing I knew I was standing on the edge of a shimmering plain through which a river wound like a silver ribbon.

In the distance a towering caldera of primitive beauty fronted by belts of trees watered by streams from glaciers above beckoned me to admire its configuration at close quarters, but it would have meant going out of my way and I had Heidi to find. People don't just disappear without trace. It was possible, of course, that she had circumvented the mire and exited the other side, driven on by guilt and fear.

*****

I went back the way I came, keeping an eye open for familiar landmarks. The terrain was new to me with thick undergrowth interspersed with carpets of grass, and a kind of giant tropical bluebell with leaves the texture of human skin. There was no shortage of wild boar. A family of about a dozen appeared in front of me. One old tusker came up close and backed off indifferently. I froze at the sound of baying dogs. The old tusker sniffed the air and carried on rooting.

The other boars ushered the sows and piglets in a bunch and formed a phalanx around them; an impenetrable shield of malignant eyes and razor-sharp tusks. If they were as mean as they looked, the dogs were in for a tough time.

Suddenly, all hell was let loose. Dogs converged from all directions, yapping and snarling. I shinned up a tree. Fangs proved no match for tusks as the thick-skinned boars pushed the dogs around like skittles, tossing and slashing as easily as slicing butter. Four dogs took the old tusker on and three paid the price. The other boars had to work harder for victory. The dogs lost ten before calling it a day, and the boars went back to their rooting.

Climbing down, I retraced my steps and hadn't gone ten yards when I knew where I was and immediately returned to the mire where I searched the surrounding area hoping for something that would give me a clue as to where Heidi was.

*****

The rotting vegetation, exuding the same macabre fascination, beckoned me as if death was the softer option. It wasn't hard to understand the 'easy way out' would be a strong inducement to someone in Heidi's state of mind. There would be no pain. Just plunge in like drowning, only unlike drowning you can't change your mind and climb back out. It would only take seconds. She would be out of sight before she could scream. It was then I was convinced I would never see her again, and it was then I lost control. I picked up the biggest rock I could find and threw it.

God knows how long I was there. Two, three hours maybe. I was wearing my watch but couldn't be bothered to check the time. I felt empty inside. Nothing mattered any more. I threw another rock.

*****

Next morning I went to the beach and walked and kept on walking, not caring whether the yacht arrived or not. The sea lapped the shore, fish of all shapes and sizes drifted in and out of the coral visible on the ocean floor, and a lone shark was feeding inshore.

There was a flurry of activity in the trees. I saw the swishing tail of a leopard as it dropped out of sight. I ran as fast as my legs could carry me: Snarls and growls mingled with coughs and shrieks, and a scream that was unmistakably human.

I crashed through the trees and Heidi fell at my feet. She was deathly pale. I cradled her head in my arms. Barks and shrieks rose up again as dozens of eyes watched us. I laid her down gently and walked towards them, fists clenched when she stopped me in my tracks. "It wasn't them. It was the leopard. They got it before it got me."

She was right on the first count and wrong on the second. Her left shoulder was badly mauled and the leopard lay dead a few yards away, its throat ripped out. She had lost a lot of blood. I cradled her head again but I was no longer there. All she could see was Danny. She reached out, and all that she felt since Danny came along and drained the life's blood from her distilled to its very essence in a cry that will haunt me for the rest of my days. "Danny. I knew I'd find you. Now we can be together, always."

She even found the strength to smile. Then she took a deep breath and passed away. The barks and shrieks subsided to wails as melancholy as before; the eyes no longer there.

I fetched the spade from the cabin and buried her in a grave as deep as I could to deter scavengers, said a little prayer and returned to the cabin.

*****

I don't know how long I was there, two, three hours maybe. I lost track of time. Nothing mattered any more; who I was, what I stood for or what I was going to do. Picking up the pieces and getting on with life was the first priority. I reflected on what might have been had I handled it differently. But no matter what I did the result would have been the same. Heidi was besotted with Danny from the word go. If he hadn't turned up perhaps her moods and indifference would have died a natural death. I'll never know. All I know is no matter what I had in mind, fate had decreed otherwise. I wanted to go way and forget but that could never be. So I did the next best thing: I went for a walk.

*****

The rainforest looked solid and impenetrable. Birds and monkeys of all shapes and sizes struck up a chorus as I passed. There was a movement in the long grass and I could only assume alligators were in the area, given there was a river close by. Then I caught sight of an equally dangerous monster, a python, which, fortunately for me went in the other direction. It had eaten and was looking for a place to sleep. Preoccupied with this and other things going on around me, I managed to put Heidi at the back of my mind. It was hard to believe she was everything I had been looking for, kind, considerate, always a kind word. But people change.

I had no intention of going back home. Pago Mara was my home as far as I was concerned. What was good enough for Elizabeth was good enough for me.

I was my own boss for the first time in my life and my new-found freedom pleased me. What would I tell my friends anyhow? That Heidi had fallen for a man who came from nowhere and died without saying who he was? It wasn't as if I had anything to lose by not going home; a boring old job as a lecturer, rented flat, a few friends and what was left of my inheritance. Certainly nothing as exciting as this; life in the raw, a constant fight for survival, get or be got. The only trick was staying alive. It is amazing that in so short a space of time I had learnt so much and was still learning.

*****

At the river's edge I heard voices. Twenty yards away was a shack with a grass roof. Three men were pottering around outside, a motley crew in ragged trousers, torn shirts and bandanas. Before I could duck down they spotted me and came over. The leader, who was everybody's idea of how a Mexican bandit should be, eyed me suspiciously. Like the baboons, the others urged him on.

He spoke with a Spanish accent. "Your name, Senor? What is your business?"

It struck me as odd that such an accent should be heard in this part of the world. This was the South Pacific, not South America, but I said nothing. I thought it wise to pretend not to understand. If I couldn't communicate I couldn't get into trouble.

The others shuffled their feet nervously, looking me up and down. The leader withdrew. I couldn't see any firearms. If they were bandits or drug smugglers they would certainly be armed. Armed or not, they were certainly up to no good. If it hadn't been for my size I think they would have killed me on the spot.

Another cleared his throat. "Vous l'avez entendu, que vouez-vous et quel est votre nom?"

French if I wasn't mistaken. I didn't understand a word he said, though I guessed he was asking the same question. I wondered what nationality the third one was. They looked at one another and then at me, muttered among themselves, turned and walked away. They glanced back once or twice. I watched them out of sight.

*****

By the time I found a suitable log to cross the river dusk was falling and a deafening chorus struck up. Toads, frogs, lizards and other reptilia gave voice to their own distinctive song. I prepared to bed down for the night. If the three men knew I was setting up camp right under the noses they might not be pleased. They might even decide to do something about it and then there would be fun and games. But it didn't come to that. As luck would have it I found a canoe half-hidden in the reeds, or, to be more correct, trapped in the reeds, and looked as if it had been there since time began. One side was damaged but it was still usable.

After scraping away faeces and other deposit accumulated over the years and dousing it in water to make it smell sweet, I sat in it testing it for size when something caught my eye. Next to my feet was a wristwatch. I picked it up. The clasp had broken. There was no inscription. I slipped it in my pocket.

*****

I felt like a smuggler of old as I eased the canoe down the sloping bank into the river under the glow of the moon. The current, stronger than I thought, tried to snatch it from my grasp. When I got used to the paddles I was skimming over the water like a true professional. Now and then a scream rang through the darkness followed by familiar barks.

Through gaps in the trees moonlight illuminated figures huddled around a flickering fire, but for the most part I was alone as I slid past in the night. I was surprised there were so many people on the island, given that reefs and cliffs made it a no-go area.

According to Irvie's map, the island was almost the size of Fiji. The reef and cliffs saved it from the modern world. No tourists - disruption; no disruption - no hassle; no hassle - no tourists, simple as that.

Situated in the South Pacific, it was hardly the place you would expect to find feuding baboons, wild boar, wild dogs, leopards, alligators and pythons that can swallow a roebuck whole.

*****

The further downstream I went the thicker the vegetation. Giant trees towered over me, their branches trailing in the water. I was careful not to in capsize. The canoe was sleek and swift but not very strong. You have to know what you're doing. But, as I said, I was learning.

The events of the past few days were taking their toll. I was tired and hungry. I had been on the go since leaving the yacht and the last meal I'd had was before meeting Danny, but no matter. You don't go forward by looking back, and if I were to survive I would not only have to forget the past but stop feeling sorry for myself. I eased the canoe into the side, secured it with vine, camouflaged it with leaves and settled down for the night in the fork of a tree.

Next morning I had fish for breakfast. I went to the

river to drink and it swam towards me begging to be eaten. I made a fire and cooked it, keeping an eye out for alligators and snakes. My perception was getting sharper, and sensing danger rather than listening for it was becoming second nature. I had never eaten fish cooked on an open fire and was surprised how tasty it was.

I dragged the canoe back into the water and kept on paddling. I had no idea where I was going nor did I care. I wouldn't report what had happened to the authorities. If no one found Heidi and Danny, no one would know. You could call it poetic justice. They died as they lived, lying and cheating.

CHAPTER EIGHT

TO THE RESCUE

I spent a week on the river, paddling by day and sleeping by night, living on fish and fruit. The rainforest thinned out and I found myself on the seacoast fronted by a blue lagoon with patches of green where anemone thrived on the coral on the bottom. Shoals of fish glided through the coral fluently and gracefully. The rolling waves and lapping breakers sang in harmony.

I sat looking out to sea thinking what a strange place to be. To find myself in such splendour, to feel the sea breeze in my face in one of the most beautiful and least populated places on earth must surely be the stuff of dreams.

Amid such beauty it seemed appropriate that I should reflect on how blind I had been. I had different ideas then; naive, you might say. I was in love for the first time and all I could see was what I wanted to see. Now my eyes were wide open and I could see things as they really were; the sun-kissed beach, the blue sweep of the ocean, palm trees waving and whispering in the breeze, wheeling gulls fighting and squabbling and flocks of migrating geese, high above, speeding relentlessly in V-formation towards the horizon.

The lagoon and ocean had their own brand of beauty; different yet the same in that each knew its place and contributes to the whole. But the thing about these two contrasting scenarios was the light. The lagoon had a lot to offer with its dramatic hues and myriad shades, whereas the ocean reflected nothing but blue in the sky above and in the depths below; nothing to focus on, nothing to exhibit but an endless expanse of blue water and infinite desolation. I returned to the canoe where I slept the night.

*****

When I awoke the next morning I was hungry. Eating fish can get boring after a time, so I had no choice but to hunt what game I could find, something I didn't look forward to. That fish were no different, that they feel pain and fight for their lives escaped me as it escapes most people. Perhaps it's because fish don't have appealing eyes and squeal pitifully like the seal and deer.

I had pork for breakfast, using the knife I had brought with me. It had an eight-inch blade, perfect for dispatching quarry quickly and painlessly. I kept it in my belt out of harm's way.

In Paradise anything can happen and it is easy to confuse illusion with reality, but it was no illusion when shafts of fluttering lights like flashing neon appeared above the tree-tops and trailed away over the ocean like plumes of smoke. They were birds island-hopping, you might say, going from island to island seeking food at the same time spreading pollen.

*****

I was on my travels again, eschewing the canoe in favour of walking, following the coastline until my feet ached. The sea breeze was welcome. It cooled me down. I hadn't forgotten Elizabeth. I would visit her grave when I was settled and more confident in where I was going.

I came to a pebble beach, probably the only pebble beach on the island, through which tracks led from the sea into the interior. The pebbles, not indigenous to the island, had been put there for a reason, probably to accommodate something heavy.

Drug smuggling sprang to mind, but that requires organisation and masses of workers and all I saw were the three men and the few stragglers through the trees. What were they doing there? Were they in co with one another? If they used the beach for whatever reason, why did they set up camp so far away? The answers to my questions came when I stumbled upon dozens of trees shorn of branches and other protuberances by the logging company ready for shipping.

The ship probably snagged the reef and went down before they could be loaded. But not to worry, the jungle was reclaiming them. They were almost swallowed up by layers of lush vegetation where they shouldn't have been taken from in the first place.

I passed on and saw schools of dolphins, basking sharks, feeding whales, gulls skimming the surface of the waves looking for food, and on the beach turtles, dozens of them.

*****

Days grew into weeks and it was then I remembered the yacht. More than four weeks had passed, five weeks to the day to be exact. My watch not only gave the time, but dates and days as well.

So much had happened it seemed like only yesterday. Heidi and Danny came back to me. The captain of the yacht might have sent a dinghy to investigate when we didn't turn up as arranged. He might even have landed on the island himself and conducted a personal search. What if he discovered the bodies? Questions would be asked. Not that I had anything to hide but some people might not agree. I tried to save them, not kill them. But then again, some people might not see it that way.

I gazed out to sea, seeing neither ship nor speck on the horizon that might be one nor drifting debris to show where one had been. All I saw was a helicopter in the distance. I felt cut off, alone, when in fact, weighing the good against the bad, I had all the company I desired and was lucky to be alive when, by all accounts, I should be dead.

All I had to do, it seemed, was reach out and take what I wanted but there is no such thing as a free lunch. Everything has its price. When my time came I would be ready. I would see if the gods were smiling on me then. Others on the island might want rid of me. They might even be planning my murder that very moment. The three men weren't very friendly, and what's to say the others were any different? If they were in co with one another it spelt trouble. But I had the baboons on my side and I knew the rainforest.

The feeling of loneliness persisted. I gazed out to sea again. It was as if the vast ocean possessed me, and all that I that stood for, my hopes, dreams, were locked away in the fathomless depths.

Deciding to return to the cabin, I retraced my steps, passing the pebble beach again. The thought struck me that it would be nice to find a boat that would take me out to sea for a change of scenery as easily as I found the canoe, but it wasn't to be. I would pick up the canoe where I had left it, return to the cabin and then go and look for Elizabeth's grave.

*****

Going back to the lagoon was slower than coming away. Don't ask me why but I got lost. It's easy to take a wrong turn when the mind is on something else even when the swell of the ocean is pounding the ears. I found myself in strange territory. But it was rainforest and I had a good idea where I was going. The sounds were not new to me. Familiar growls and snorts greeted me with every step.

The deeper into the interior I ventured, the denser the vegetation, so I withdrew and went back way I came so as not to get lost a second time. I had learnt when looking for Heidi to keep an eye on the way I had come by looking for leaves I had disturbed, twigs I had broken or mulch I had flattened into the forest floor.

But, would you believe, I took another wrong turn and found myself climbing uphill without actually being aware of it until I was looking down on the rainforest below, though I hadn't strayed for I could see the sea and the lagoon above the tree-tops, and hear the song of the surf lapping the shore and the cries of the gulls rising and falling in harmony as breaker after breaker dashed itself to pieces on the coral.

*****

By now I was beginning to feel like a native, no better and no worse than the others. I slept the same, ate the same and killed if I had to. But I still washed and kept myself clean if only to remind myself I was human. I would change into fresh clothes when I got back to the cabin. As for shaving: I didn't have a razor but what I did have was a fine beard.

I was on my way back down to ground level when I heard a cry coming from a thicket ahead of me. Then a familiar growl followed. I ran as fast as I could. Behind the thicket, trying desperately to climb a tree, was a young woman sobbing and screaming, her finger-nails broken from trying to scale the slippery trunk. When she saw me she sank to her knees and screamed again, her eyes transfixed on something to my left. I turned my head. It was a leopard. I froze, knowing that a sudden movement might be my last. The other I took by surprise but not this one. It was puzzled by my indifference and lack of fear.

I was getting used to the ways of animals by now and knew that when faced with the unexpected they either attack or retreat. There are no half measures but this one proved the exception. I met its baleful gaze and clenched my fists prepared for the worst but it was still trying to figure me out, as bewildered as the baboon was. As the most feared predator on the island, it was not used to being defied, let alone challenged by someone who refused to be intimidated. It simply did not know what to do.

The woman neither, whose screams reduced to sobs. Then swiftly and silently, the leopard disappeared into the undergrowth. And just as suddenly the woman ran into my arms, blinded by tears. Heidi had done the same, only this time the woman didn't think I was someone else.

"You're very brave," she cried. "You came just in time. What's your name?" She spoke good English.

I got a good look at her. She had delicately features, dusky brown skin, raven-black hair and looked every bit the Queen of the Island. All that was missing was a sarong and a garland in her hair. As it was she wore a skirt of sorts halfway up her thighs that made her easier on the eye than she was already, but admiration was the last thing she wanted and I wasn't in the mood either.

Attached to her wrist was a small leather pouch she kept grasping as an assurance that it was still there. Her teeth were dreams to smile with but she wasn't smiling now. I looked into her upturned eyes and it was like looking into her soul: Vulnerable, crying inside. An excited chorus of coughs and barks came from the canopy above. Dozens of eyes looked down, and one by one they went away.

She snuggled up close. "Who are they?" she cried.

I smiled. "Friends, just friends."

"I don't understand."

I smiled again. "You're not meant to. What's your name?"

"Cora."

"Mine's Kieron."

She relaxed a little and cheered up. I wouldn't admit it at the time, not even to myself, that I could have had held her all day. But it wasn't my idea. I didn't ask her to come along. It might have been divine intervention to find out whether I was a good protector and provider. Anything's possible. All I knew was her name. I didn't know where she was from or what brought her here, and she knew less about me. What struck me as odd was she wasn't afraid as if being alone with a stranger in a place where life and death hung in the balance, but enough of that. What was important was survival, and in order to achieve it I must put all other notions I might have at the back of my mind.

*****

I resumed my travels taking her with me. I picked up

the canoe and took to the river again. The current was against us but I knew what I was doing. I couldn't take my eyes off her. Where Heidi was a natural show off, Cora was modesty personified, cute rather than pretty. She laughed as I struggled to keep the canoe on a straight course. I laughed too although it was no laughing matter.

It was refreshing to meet someone who didn't have all the troubles in the world and wanted everybody in the world to share them. Not that I planned to make it more than it was but I was curious all the same. Maybe she was curious about me.

Settling into my usual rhythm, I skimmed over the water swiftly and silently as we dodged the usual overhead branches trailing in the water. She pointed out the various fruits as we passed; melons, guavas, cocoanuts, bananas, breadfruit, red apples, melons, plums, mangoes, you name it, advising me not to eat what the monkeys didn't eat. There was no end to what she knew, which made me suspect she was more than she seemed. I guessed she was from one of the other islands, if not I would have met others of her kind, but then it was a big island and I had barely scratched the surface. Who knows what other surprises lay ahead of me? Dusk was falling. I pulled into the side and made shelter for the night.

*****

We had separate mats of dry grass to sleep on, placed side by side. I turned my back on her, partly because I respected her privacy and partly to assure her that I wouldn't take advantage of the situation when, miracles of miracles, her hand touched mine. I thought I was dreaming but it was real all right. She didn't waste time. No one expressed more clearly in terms of erotic action the delights of seductive guile, the undertones of gentle persuasion and the tendency towards uninhibited, unashamed sexual appeasement than Cora, who turned the unthinkable into the inevitable and whose stock in trade was surprise.

My determination to keep my distance wilted under a body that yielded to the touch, lips that sought mine, breathless whispers and lingering sighs. We were lovers and that was the last thing on my mind but I'm not complaining.

CHAPTER NINE

CORA GOES MISSING

I awoke the next morning to a dawn chorus of twittering birds and chattering monkeys. It was seven o'clock. Cora was sleeping, her hair seductively hiding one side of her face. I looked at her in a way I wouldn't dream of looking before. It was as if I was seeing her for the first time and found myself liking her perhaps more than I should. But isn't that what lovers are supposed to do?

Up to then I hadn't taken a great deal of notice and didn't consider her as anything other than an attractive travelling companion, least of all someone capable of stirring emotions I thought had died long ago. Infatuation? Your guess is as good as mine? I let her sleep and made a fire of twigs and dry grass to be topped up with logs later, and went looking for food but not before boarding up the entrance so she would be safe.

*****

I left the canoe and followed the river on foot, knowing that if I didn't catch fish I would get other food. Anything is better than nothing. There was the tang of ozone in the air so we weren't far from the sea. Perhaps, subconsciously, I was drawn to it. After all, it is a where it all began: Stepping ashore with Heidi, holding hands, finding the cabin and then bingo - Danny turned up and ruined everything. But that was in the past and best forgotten.

There was a movement in the trees. A young boar, blinded by panic, ran towards me and then veered off at the last minute. I could have had it for breakfast but let it pass. Showing Cora I was no better than the leopard might have an adverse affect so early in our relationship, so I decided we'd have fruit for breakfast and let her find out for herself that it was kill or be killed. But she probably knew that already.

*****

Living out in the open is okay if you can stand the elements. Rain or shine was all the same to me. The beauty of it is there are no deadlines to meet, no one to answer to, as free as a bird to marvel at the beauty, the sheer grandeur and majesty at the side of which civilisation, with all its pomp and synthetic splendour, pales into insignificance. The dictum 'what you see is what you get' is what the eco-system is all about, where each knows its place and God help those who step out of line. Why I was allowed to roam with impunity is a matter of conjecture. Perhaps it was because I adhered to the rules and gave as good as I got. I was even allowed to pick up a few friends along the way. They followed me everywhere, watching and waiting.

*****

On my way back I smelt smoke. Cora had been busy. She had built up the fire and was toasting fish on a stick in the way you toast bread. How she caught the fish was anybody's guess since this stretch of river was like the Grand Rapids, and then I saw a length of vine to which thorns were attached at intervals. I had heard of such a method of fishing where the vine is cast downstream and pulled against the current thereby hooking any fish that gets in its way. Simple but effective.

All she said was, "You're late."

If I expected more I was in for a disappointment. She didn't even ask where I'd been as if there was nothing between us. Maybe there wasn't. Or maybe she was shy or disappointed or both, or it was no big deal and I was making something out of nothing. Chances are she hadn't prepared breakfast just for me because maybe she was hungry herself. I didn't know what to think.

When the fish was cooked I passed her the knife and she cut it in half and gave me a piece. Palm leaves served as plates. It tasted better than I expected perhaps because it was as if I hadn't eaten in years.

"Nice, but I'd give my right arm for egg and bacon," I said.

"I owe you an explanation," she began.

I cocked my ears. "I'm listening."

"Sorry about last night."

It sounded so funny I felt like laughing. "Why, what happened?"

There was a throb in her voice. "You know."

"I will when you tell me."

"You were a gentleman throughout."

"You're quite a lady yourself."

"I was. I'm not now. I took advantage."

This time I did laugh. "You what?"

"Took advantage," she repeated. "You were tired, your resistance was low. You risked your life for me and I repaid you by exploited your vulnerability for my own selfish needs."

"Is that what you call it?"

Her eyelashes brushed her cheeks. "I don't think it's funny."

I laughed again. "I do. Anything else you want to apologise for?"

She still didn't think it funny. "Can you ever forgive me?"

"I'll try."

"I want you to like me. You do like me, don't you?"

"If it's that important, yes, I like you."

She needed reassuring. "You don't think any less of me?"

I wanted to take her in my arms but remembered the last time I took a woman in my arms. "Why should I? I was as much part of it as you. It takes two to tango."

She looked relieved. "Thank you. That's all I wanted to hear." She kissed me. "That's for saving my life, I'll never forget you. I must go now. I'll see you again some time," and with that she disappeared through the trees.

*****

I ticked off the minutes. She didn't return. To say I was miffed is an understatement. She could have at least told me she wasn't coming back and looked sad about it even if she didn't mean it. But where would she go? Then I remembered we were in the rainforest. Anything can happen in a rainforest. I was a fool to let her go. Maybe it was her way of having fun and only intended to go for a walk when a leopard had hold of her, or wild dogs or the baboons? No, not the baboons, they were my friends. As far as they were concerned Cora was my woman. Didn't I save her from the leopard? Would I have done so otherwise? Of course I would but the baboons didn't know that.

I searched far and wide, calling her name, making as much noise as possible to let her know I was there if needed. Even the forest fell silent. In a way it seemed as if the past twelve hours had never happened and Cora was a dream, a figment of my imagination. But she wasn't a dream.

She was real all right, as real as the fish she cooked, the fishing line, the bed of grass she slept on and a night I would never forget.

I wouldn't give up. I would move heaven and earth until I found her. I knew some of the island, and what I didn't know I would soon learn. The question uppermost in my mind was if she hadn't been abducted or prevented from returning, what other reason could she have had for leaving the way she did? Not because I took advantage of her. She took advantage of me, she said so.

*****

I searched until I was exhausted. I'm sure the baboons lent a hand because every now and I caught sight of one looking down at me from the branches. I didn't see a leopard, wild dog or pig though. Perhaps they had heard of me and gave me a wide berth. News travels. But I saw other animals. They were my friends. They were all my friends, it's just the leopards I didn't get along with.

I continued the search into the following week. If Heidi was worth looking for, so was she. After all, it was only an island. There are limits to how long you can remain hidden on an island. If she had gone back to her people I would find her. All I had to do was keep looking. I missed her more than I would admit; her smile, the way she looked at me, the nuances and peculiarities that go unnoticed until they are no longer there.

I went back to the canoe and paddled a little before letting it drift as I looked around me. It was then I saw my first alligator. It came up close. I shouted my loudest and it went away. Where there was one, there were many. I feared more would follow and was relieved when they didn't. What they do, I've been told, is capsize a canoe and rip the threshing passengers to pieces. Nonsense, but I kept close to the shoreline just in case.

When I came to the shack where I saw the three men, I hoped they didn't see me. They would only want the canoe back and there would be a fight and they would get hurt and I didn't want that. They could have their canoe when I was good and ready, not before. Not looking where I was going I turned into a tributary. I was in strange territory. No one was watching over me. They were but not now.

I was alone save for the usual multi-coloured birds and myriad tree-life that gazed at me wondering what kind of creature I was. It was a struggle turning the canoe against the current and getting back on track.

Further along the river narrowed, carrying vegetation and debris in the fast undertow. I was making good time. But you can only make good time if you've somewhere to go. I had nowhere to go except the cabin and Elizabeth's grave.

CHAPTER TEN

THE RETURN JOURNEY

I went off course again but it wasn't my fault this time. Turbulence forced the canoe into a creek so overgrown with trees it was like going into a tunnel. I saw no life in the branches but that didn't mean no life was there.

Unknowingly, I was paddling blindly towards marshland and had almost passed the point of no return when shafts of daylight streaming through the canopy warned of danger ahead. Turning the canoe round was harder than the last time. It meant pushing it waist-high in the filthiest water I have seen. I lost my footing and went under a couple of times, and when I finally emerged into the daylight I cleaned myself as best I could but I wasn't complaining. I was only too glad to be alive.

In no time I was on the move again. The silence was deafening. All I could hear was the splash of the paddles as they sliced through the water, and strangely, paddling behind me. I looked back and saw nothing. Then I thought I heard laughter. I listened. Likewise nothing. I pulled myself together. I was hallucinating. A sixth-sense warning me that something was about to happen was real enough though, and I had no choice but to wait until it happened by which time it might be too late. But nothing did.

It seemed I was spending most of my time chasing people. First Heidi, then Danny and now Cora. Did they find me so repellent or was it coincidence that, whether by accident or design, they finished up avoiding me but the baboons didn't avoid me, they were my friends.

*****

In the afternoon I tied the canoe to a tangle of roots and stepped ashore into thick mud, scattering small mud-skipping fish and freshwater crabs that scuttled into their burrows. I sat in the shade of a tree, took off my shoes and cleaned them. Sweat poured off me. There was no respite from the heat except the river, and plunging in was out of the question since it was more dangerous than dry land.

I knew if I was going to make the island my home I had to have a plan of some sort instead of wandering aimlessly up and down feeling sorry for myself. It wasn't my idea to play Tarzan, it just happened. Now if I could only find Cora, and she was willing, we could set up home together in the cabin and take it from there. I would visit Elizabeth's grave in my own good time, and if Cora was of the same mind so could come along too. Whatever her reaction it would be nothing compared to the jeering response elicited from Heidi if I had told her. I might be wrong, of course, and Cora might respond similarly, but it was conjecture too absurd to merit consideration. I didn't know where Cora was and might never know.

*****

I had covered some of the island since leaving the cabin, not as much as I liked but it was early days. I wouldn't be satisfied until I knew more, taking in a bit at a time, memorising landmarks, short cuts and which areas to avoid and which not to avoid. But first I would return to the cabin and freshen up a little. The food the captain had given us wouldn't go to waste. It wouldn't all be fit to eat, of course. What wasn't I would throw away. If I remember correctly there was tinned ham, baked beans and tomatoes.

I had been travelling for what seemed a lifetime but it wouldn't take long to make the return journey. I was halfway there already. I would travel the rest of the way inland instead of following the coast that is exposed with nowhere to hide. In the rainforest there are thousands of places to hide. Besides, I missed my friends the baboons. Let's hope they missed me.

*****

Leaving the canoe again, I turned to earth's magnetic field for guidance, having had the foresight to bring the compass with me, and made my way to the nearest forest, which was worse than most.

Light filtering through the canopy made dappled patterns across the green leaves of the understorey, and ended glowing white on the trampled leaves on the floor below. Insects were everywhere, on my clothes, in my hair, and the more I brushed them away the thicker they became. And if it wasn't insects it was tiny midges that cling to the skin and suck you dry, or attractive blooms sprouting from branches that sting when touched, grow legs and run away. Not only do they use disguises, but also many species enter into an alliance with other animals and plants in a kind of evolutionary mutual protection society to such an extent their lives become intricately entwined.

Common also are climbing evergreens that can strangle you, innocuous-looking leaves that sting you and roots guaranteed to break your ankles; and once down the odds are you won't get back up again. All in all a hellish place to be, requiring savvy and a certain amount of luck not to succumb to these dangers and others that lay in wait for the unwary, including, worst of all, getting lost. If you think the easy way out is to climb a tree, you will be welcomed by numerous biting and stinging creatures from bees to scorpions living in the plants that cling to the bark. This, added to the inevitable vertigo, is enough to ensure humans keep their feet on the ground. I was lucky. I learnt how to circumvent impenetrable thickets without going too far out of my way.

This was the big test. If I could tackle this, I could tackle anything. The only thing going for it, according to the map, was it was a short cut. The other way was back the way I came. This way would cut my journey by half. All I had to do was stay alive.

*****

At last I emerged into glorious sunshine and followed a well-trodden path made by an animal much larger than I had encountered, and was asking myself what manner of animal it might be when a white-faced, red-flanked Hereford bull, usually seen grazing in English meadows, stepped out in front of me.

I thought I was hallucinating again when it snorted and pawed the ground as if it knew what I was thinking. At first it wouldn't let me pass, and I was about to put my circumventing skills to the test when it stepped to one side and let me be on my way. I can only assume it was because I didn't pose a threat. I was both relieved and startled. Relieved that it showed such a remarkable capacity for appreciating my position and startled that it should be there in the first place.

I consulted the compass and map frequently as I headed back south. Elizabeth's grave was further north in the interior while Newtown was a mere two-hour journey on the west coast where the river spilled into the sea. I would visit them both at my leisure. I had the rest of my life in front of me. I hadn't forgotten Cora. If anything happened to her ...I clenched my fists.

For the first time I was seized by a great panic as though the rainforest, rivers and mountains were the very things that imprisoned me. I was in an inhabited wilderness with a culture that had taken thousands of years to develop, and there I was, a relative newcomer, strutting around as if I owned the place when in fact I amounted to very little no matter how much I proclaimed myself king. I was the same as the others, no better, no worse, and mustn't forget it. The moment I did I was finished.

*****

It didn't take as long as I thought to get back to the cabin. The first thing I noticed was the mound of soil where I buried the fawn. The soil hadn't flattened while I had been away and was freshly turned as if it had been dug that morning. The ashes where I had burned the dogs had blown away. It was hard to believe I had been away five months. In a passing flight of fancy I thought how nice it would be to have had the fawn as a pet but that was impossible. Anyhow, it was too young to be away from its mother and would have died anyway.

*****

The cabin was big enough to house twenty men as

I found out when I counted the beds and lockers I didn't notice when I moved in with Heidi. Also there were tables, chairs, food cupboard, first-aid kit, pot-bellied stove, gas rings with calor gas bottles, pots, pans, cutlery, sink with drainage but no running water, playing-cards, books and sundry other things on the window-sills I didn't notice either. I was too preoccupied with what was going on between her and Danny to notice anything.

My suspicion that the logging company had used it to house its employees was confirmed when I found letterheads, trade magazines and newspapers etc. The first thing I did was making the cabin look less like a junkyard and more like home. So far, so good. Everything was going according to plan. The only thing bugging me was Cora. Where could she be?

I must have dozed off because the next thing I knew dusk was falling. I went outside. Familiar grunts and barks greeted me. I noted the clearing had shrunk since I was last there and getting smaller as if the rainforest had speeded up reclaiming it, knowing I was coming back. I had the necessary tools left by the cabin's previous occupants so there was no excuse not to do something about it.

I spotted several rusty old drums poking out from the raised floor of the cabin between the brick struts it stood on. I could hear liquid splashing around as I picked one up and took it inside. It took me ages to get the top off. It was paraffin, and where there was paraffin there were lamps. I rummaged around and found half a dozen in a scuttle where they kept the logs. There were no logs. I would have to get some. At night it was freezing cold, and I would be very surprised if the gas in the bottles hadn't evaporated over the years. I wondered how

Elizabeth kept warm at night but she was used to it. I was still learning.

*****

The next morning I swept the cabin floor and noticed blood where the leopard killed Danny. Luckily it had spilled on a carpet that I burned. Next I cleaned the windows and was stuffing blankets and pillows into a cupboard when I came across a chest with metal bands and studded corners like a pirate's chest. I fancied it contained hidden treasure when in fact it contained nothing but old newspapers and magazines. But it didn't stop me dreaming.

What a turn up for the books it would be if it had been hidden treasure. Treasure in the tropics, a crock of gold on my Island of Dreams. Nice work if you can get it. But who wants wealth? Wealth attracts people and people spell trouble. My crock of gold was just being there. All that was missing was Cora. My next find cheered me up no end; axes and machetes, handy for cutting a trail in the bush and keeping the encroaching jungle at bay.

I soon got into a routine, and it was as if I had never been away: Fresh fruit in the morning, a dip the river river where it was shallow and easy to spot lurking alligators, and the rest of the day hacking away at the encroaching jungle. Wildfowl formed the main part of my diet. They were easy to catch. Killing them was quick and painless. I tried living on fruit so I wouldn't have to kill but lost weight and was ill for a week. I threw out the rancid butter and other perishables unfit to eat. There was plenty of tea and coffee but only a few cans of baked beans, No big deal. I had gone without baked beans before and could go without them again.

Although I only got an occasional glimpse of the baboons, I knew they were watching, ever vigilant, ready to warn me of the slightest danger. As time went by they made forays into the clearing, getting bolder with each visit but keeping their distance. Whether it was fear that I might harm them or respect for my privacy, I couldn't say. Bearing in mind that familiarity breeds contempt, I didn't encourage them but I was glad of their company all the same.

One incident sticks in my mind as if it was only yesterday. I was chopping logs when I heard the most calamitous din you could imagine. I ran as fast as I could in the direction of the cabin. A fight was taking place between two male baboons, urged on by excited spectators. They couldn't have been fighting for more than a couple of minutes but already the fight was in the subservience stage, with one strutting victoriously and smacking his lips loudly, and the other signalling defeat with a kind of nervous grin and raising its tail vertically.

When they saw me the fight was forgotten and they disappeared into the trees like naughty children. I did my best to convey that no offence would be taken provided it didn't happen again. They seemed to understand for they came back in twos and threes and stood around looking guilty. In my position it didn't pay to make enemies.

*****

Rainstorms were frequent and followed a familiar pattern. First thunder, then the sky went black and rain came down with a vengeance, flattening, bending and then stopping as suddenly as it started. They were either over in ten minutes or lasted all day. At the first sign of a storm the baboons left the camp and headed for home as quickly as they could, obviously feeling safer among the rocks. That was the only time the camp was completely deserted.

*****

It took me the best part of three weeks to get the clearing back to size, hacking, chopping and cutting. The baboons' visits grew less frequent until they stopped coming altogether, then a week later they were back to normal. Other monkeys took their place during their absence and stayed. One was bold enough to perch on the cabin roof to get a better view. It amused me that I was the centre of attraction.

I marked off the boundary with a bamboo fence, one metre high and three hundred metres in circumference with gaps at regular intervals for egress and ingress, not so much to keep out trespassers as to proclaim it as my territory. The baboons were interested spectators who kept in touch old like friends who don't want to be forgotten.

My endeavours to fit in and adherence to the rules were at last beginning to bear fruit. After such a arduous apprenticeship I could now call myself a true denizen of the rainforest who fitted in as well as the next. I marked off the calendar. To my surprise I had been on the island six months.

CHAPTER ELEVEN

HOME SWEET HOME

My favourite time was late evening relaxing outside the cabin in the glow of the moon. The rustle of the trees and hum of forest life blended harmoniously. If it was cold I stayed in the cabin and passed the time reading a book or simply lying down thinking. The funny thing is I didn't miss television or other trappings of civilisation, but it would have been nice to have the radio Danny was playing if only to remind me of home. But this was my home and I wouldn't exchange it for the world. Even if I did find the radio, the battery would be flat anyway.

The curtains at the windows in the part of the cabin I didn't use I kept closed while the others I opened by day to let in the daylight. It was these that proved a chore, opening and closing to the dictates of dawn and dusk, but I had no choice. Leaving them open at night would attract more inquisitive eyes than moths to a light bulb. The monkeys were the boldest and would have pulled faces at me with their noses pressed to the glass twenty-four hours a day if I let them.

But it wasn't all leisure and ease. I had fits of depression in which I was convinced nothing I did was worthwhile; that I didn't amount to much, my achievements were failures and what I had wasn't worth having. And it was during one of these spells that I discovered the Bible; a book I wouldn't normally read but in the circumstances perfectly normal. It taught me to think less about myself and more about others, especially those who didn't have what I had: The freedom to come and go as I please, and good health. But I wasn't completely without pain. What I needed was company, and what better company than Cora? If I found her I would never let her go.

*****

Rested and fighting fit, I decided it was time to visit Elizabeth's grave and explore the rest of the island. With luck I might run into Cora. I might even run into the three men. If I did, and, like the baboons, they got in my way, I would bowl them over like skittles and go about my business. I planned to set out early the next morning, armed with the map, compass, machete, axe and the knife; a ritual that had become part of me. I went nowhere without them.

*****

The following morning I shaved off my beard, had breakfast, bathed in the river and rummaged through the few clothes I had brought with me: Jeans, shirts, swimming trunks, razors, floppy hat that shielded my eyes from the sun, sandals, two pairs of shoes and a pair of boots described as 'safari boots' by the salesman who sold them to me; soft uppers, leather souls and steel toe-caps. I hoped they lived up to their name. To tell you the truth I had forgotten them. The shoes I was wearing were threadbare and ripped to pieces but comfortable. I seldom took them off. In the rainforest you can't take anything off without someone moves in and claims it as its own.

I burned Heidi's belongings, not out of spite but for a number of reasons, one being if a search party came looking for us they wouldn't find anything that would raise questions that couldn't be answered.

*****

The baboons came to wish me luck, knowing I was leaving. They even staged a ceremony in my honour, moving backwards and forwards in an ungainly, shuffling gait, their doglike faces set grotesquely as they shrieked and howled inharmoniously. Then they regrouped, the young ones in front and the older ones behind. It was touching to see these strange creatures sitting and acting like dogs, even displaying the same adulation and patience. I was lucky to have them as friends, and knew they would take care of things for me.

I changed into a pair of jeans, clean shirt, underwear, jungle boots and tried a lumberjack's belt on for size. Made of thick leather, it had loops for carrying tools. I couldn't have wished for more.

*****

I was on the point of departure when closely-packed spiky-barked chontas trees caught my eye to the rear of the cabin, and I wondered what lay behind them. Probably nothing but I had to be sure. Although my faith in the baboons was unshakable, it would, nevertheless, be foolish to leave without taking every precaution to ensure my home would be doubly safe while I was away.

Impossible to climb, the chontas discouraged contact, human or otherwise, and woe betide anyone who ignored their warning. I made my way between them as if they might leap out and eat me, exited the other side, got carried away by the exotic flora before me and went further than I intended.

The landscape changed dramatically. I felt a sudden chill when I found myself in a salurian park, older than time itself. At my feet was an outcrop of needle-sharp volcanic rock that reached upwards of some fifteen metres studded with marine fossils, brachionops and suchlike from ancient seas. A place creaking with age but still going strong. My dream, hopes and purpose in life were pretty insignificant in comparison. I felt humbled.

As if that wasn't enough I was shown another side of what I was and what I stood for when a rock fell from above and missed me by inches. I had won the respect of all who knew me, ready to help those less fortunate than myself, always there when needed yet I amounted to nothing. My life had been spared by the blind chance of a rock not falling on me. It gave me a new perspective of life and what it meant.

*****

I postponed setting out until the following morning and did nothing for the rest of the day. I didn't sleep that night and paced up and down until the first light of dawn. The usual early morning chorus struck up but I wasn't listening. Then sleep overtook me. I slumped down on the bed, closed my eyes and was out for the count.

I awoke with a start to the sound of coughs and barks. I leapt off the bed and looked out of the window. The three men emerged into the clearing carrying rifles. A baboon was halfway across the clearing on its way to warn me and was shot. It rolled over clutching its stomach, writhing in agony and was shot again. Then the men sprayed the trees with bullets and three more baboons fell to their deaths, among them a baby whose mother met the same fate when she came to its rescue. Then they fired at anything that moved before making their way in my direction.

I put the knife in my belt and clambered out of a window on the other side of the cabin where they wouldn't see me and crouched down where I could see their feet under the raised floor. The leader's feet disappeared up the steps that led to the door, came back up and barked out an order whereupon the other two went in opposite directions circumventing the cabin with me in the middle.

I had to think fast. I ran to the nearest corner and waited. As the first man turned I took him by the throat, twisted and broke his neck, and knocked the other one out as he turned the other corner. It was only a matter of time before the leader got the same. I threw the rifles in a heap and waited for the last two to recover.

*****

When they came to, they got to their feet and gasped as the sight of their dead pal, and then went deathly pale as the baboons emerged from the trees on all fours yelping and pulling faces.

"Stop them, have mercy," the leader cried. "We are sorry for what we did but it was either kill or be killed."

"Liar," I retorted. "I was watching from the window. You killed them for no other reason than they were there. What do you expect them to do, pat you on the back? I think it only fair I give them their revenge."

He got down on his knees. "No, Senor, anything but that. They will tear us to pieces. We will do anything you say."

I signalled the baboons to keep their distance. A young male kept coming with the intention of getting it over with. I exhorted him to be patient. His reply was to bare his fangs in a terrible display of bottled up fury before bowing to my authority and resuming his place in the ranks.

"For God's sake, Senor," the leader cried again, "don't let him have us. It will be murder."

"No more than what you did to his brothers and sisters," I reminded him, "or is it that everyone is equal except the baboons are a little less equal? If so, tell them that. I don't think they'd understand. They're family. Harm one and you harm them all."

The other started blubbering. The leader showed his contempt by telling him to shut up, and shut up himself when the young male went up on its hind legs as if telling me it was his brethren the men had killed therefore it should be left to them to decide their fate.

"What are you doing in this part of the world?" I queried.

The leader replied, "We go any place where there is work."

"You won't find work here," I told him.

They glanced at each other and the look in their eyes told me all I wanted to know.

I asked another question. "You're on the run. Who from?"

"You've got us wrong, Senor," the leader cried. "We have done nothing. Our passports were stolen and we were afraid we would be sent back to South America."

"What's wrong with South America?" I asked.

"There is nothing wrong with South America, Senor. South America is our home."

"In that case," I pointed out, "why don't you want to go back there?"

"It is boring, nothing to do all day. We want excitement, to travel the world. That is why we are here."

"Liar," I snapped. "What did you do, rob a bank?"

More glances, more lies. "No, Senor, our passports were stolen and that is the truth."

I was losing my patience. "You wouldn't know the truth if it leapt out and bit you. I won't ask you again. What did you do?"

Their eyes were drawn to baboons, which enraged the young male further.

"He is going to attack," the leader cried. "You will save us, yes?"

The other one spoke for the first time. He was Hispanic too. "If we tell you what you want to know, you will go to the police, no?"

Before I could reply they lunged at me. I wasn't surprised. I wasn't surprised either when they didn't put up much of a fight. I knocked them spark out. When they regained consciousness they not only looked foolish, they were foolish for even thinking they could take me on.

I ordered them to stay where they were, took the rifles to the cabin and threw them a shovel each. "Here, take these, dig two holes, one for my friends and one for your pal. He's not fit to share the same grave."

They didn't argue. It took them all afternoon. They were a sorrier sight when they finished than when they started. I ordered them to lower the baboon's bodies into the larger hole gently, and throw their pal's body into the other hole and cover them both over. Sweat poured off them. One wiped his face on a grubby handkerchief and passed it to his pal who did the same. The baboons left in twos and threes.

I addressed the other one. "You were saying?"

"We will tell you what you want to know, Senor"

"I'm listening."

The leader let him do the talking.

"You are right, Senor, we robbed a bank and killed a guard. We are not proud of what we did. Then we stole a boat and came here. We did not think it was inhabited. We thought we would be safe. We had a friend, big like you. He disappeared," he snapped his fingers, "just like that."

"Where did he go?" I asked.

"We have no idea, Senor. He went for a walk and didn't come back. We think he is dead."

"What makes you think he is dead?"

He looked around him. "This is an island, Senor. There is no escape. He was alone. He didn't come back. We have seen leopards."

"Numbers don't always guarantee safety," I said. "Look what happened to you two. Did he have a name?"

"Si Senor, he had a name. His name was Danny."

I kept my thoughts to myself. "Did he come from South America too?"

"No, Senor, Australia. It was his idea to rob the bank. He said it would be easy."

"And you think he's dead?"

"What else can he be, Senor? If he wasn't he would be here."

They glanced at each other.

I watched them closely. "He is here," I said.

His voice fell like a flat penny. "What did you say, Senor?"

"He plays a mouth organ."

"Senor?"

"Mouth organ. You know." I cupped my hands over my mouth and blew.

His smile was all teeth and no humour. "You've met him!"

"That's right. I met him, and so did a leopard. The leopard killed him and I killed the leopard."

"You killed a leopard!" they both exclaimed.

"It was either him or me. Where did you get the canoe?"

The leader took over. "What canoe?"

I answered the question with another question. "How much did you get from the bank?"

"We got nothing, Senor, and that is the truth."

I couldn't hide my disgust. "You don't place a lot of value on life, do you?" I looked at each in turn. "I'll tell you what I'm going to do. I'm going to let you go. You're free to walk out of here."

They didn't move.

The leader etched a picture of abject fear. "You mean you are setting us free here, Senor?"

"Why not, it's as good a place as any? That's what you want, isn't it?"

The silence was resonant of rustling leaves. Dozens of eyes, studious, silent, unseen, watched us across the clearing and shadows like ghosts flitted among the trees.

"But it will be murder!" he cried. "That it what they want you to do. They are waiting for us. At least let us stay until they have gone."

I shook my head. "They won't go until they've got you. You had your fun, now they want theirs."

I was heartless, without mercy, but then the jungle was a good teacher and I an eager pupil.

"At least give us weapons to defend ourselves," they pleaded.

"Why should I? The baboons didn't have weapons, Now get."

They cut a pathetic picture as they stumbled across the clearing. The leaves rustled some more. A single bark rang out followed by blood-curdling screams.

CHAPTER TWELVE

ON MY TRAVELS AGAIN

That night I slept soundly, awoke at nine the next morning and prepared myself for the long journey ahead. Two hours later I was on my way. No one was there to see me off. Leastways, that's how it looked but I knew different.

No matter what reservations I may have had regarding the journey - whether Elizabeth's grave was still there or finding myself in a predicament I couldn't get out of - I consoled myself with the thought that at least my cabin would be safe. But, to tell you the truth, I couldn't envisage a situation I couldn't get out of, or if I did wouldn't admit it. Either way, I knew I wouldn't have the baboons to watch out for me. They were fiercely territorial and would accompany me part of the way and no further unless they had to.

*****

The change in me over the past six months was startling. Apart from the occasional fit of depression and soul searching, I was wiser, fitter and happier. Not that I wasn't fit before but I felt better in myself. Fulfilled, you might say, a dream come true, and it wasn't a dream I would wake up from. It was real, actually happening. Whether by accident or design, I had achieved a lifestyle much easier than I imagined at a price no higher than effort and determination.

I frequently felt blessed and privileged at how easily

I had adapted to a scenario that would give the normal man nightmares. Whether it was by the grace of God, I wasn't sure. Nor was I sure whether I was spared for whatever reason the hardship usually associated with relying on one's own resourcefulness and initiative in the wild, or whether it was blind luck. All I know is that at one time it seemed as if the whole world was against me, and then bingo, things were fine. But I mustn't get too complacent. One wrong move could be my last.

*****

I was soon on my way, and it was only when I came to the shack the three men had occupied that things started to happen. I opened the door and stepped inside. The smell was overpowering. Sacking was spread out on the floor. Pieces of wood nailed together served as a table as did three stools constructed in similar fashion. Insects crawled over discarded scraps of food and fat spiders picked over the bones of dead flies. Stubs of candles placed strategically provided the light. I had seen all I wanted to and left the way I came.

Outside, I could see where they had tried to till the soil to grow vegetables but only managed to scratch the surface. I wasn't surprised. The soil was like concrete. While credit was due to them for trying to be self-sustaining in their efforts to remain hidden and not be brought to book for their crime, they shouldn't have committed the crime in the first place, but then, given that they did, why risk everything by trying to kill me when all they had to lose sleep over was their conscience? It didn't make sense. I nosed around. They had cut back the brush between the shack and the jungle but had no idea what to cut and what to leave alone.

I was about to continue my journey when something caught my eye; a piece of material snagged on a thicket near the path that led to the river. I examined it. If I wasn't mistaken it was the same material as Cora's skirt. A flush of hope surged through me. I was happy and angry at the same time. Happy that I might be seeing her again, and angry with whoever had abducted her and held her against her will. If she didn't leave voluntarily, that is. Heidi did, why shouldn't she? But I didn't think so. They were as different as chalk and cheese. Heidi was a flirt; Cora wouldn't know where to begin. Voluntarily or not, it was a long way from where she had disappeared.

I continued on my way. The splash of water reached my ears I didn't recall hearing the last time I was there. It turned out to an expanse of water too small to be called a pond and not big enough to be a lake I didn't recall seeing either. Roebuck and babirusa, a wild pig characterised by the extraordinary development of its canine teeth which grow through the skin of the snout and curves backwards over the forehead, were slaking their thirst at the water's edge, at peace with the world and with each another. I took a drink myself, rested and passed on.

*****

The canoe was where I left it, and it wasn't long before I was skimming over the water again. I savoured the exotic scents and sounds I didn't notice the first time I came this way. My mind was filled with more pressing problems to notice anything. I was making good progress but, as I said, time was not of the essence.

I settled into my usual rhythm, dipping the paddles into the water with the smooth, measured ease of a professional. The deeper I ventured into the interior the more I felt the jungle was closing in on me. This was the first tropical island I had visited, let alone make it my home, and its fickleness never ceased to amaze me. One minute it was rainforest, the next shimmering savannah, then rocky outcrop then marshland then rainforest again.

*****

Force of habit and an acute instinct for danger took over as my mind reflected on the change in me my adventures and new life had brought about. I had always been able to take care of myself because of my size, but size doesn't amount to much when a leopard can take prey much larger than itself yet a baboon, about the same size, puts up sufficient fight to make the leopard think twice about taking it on.

If I say I comforted my mind with hope, it is true to say that I compared my present life with the life I left behind; regular hours, meals on time, being told what to eat and what not to eat, when to sleep and when not to sleep. Here I could indulge what I liked, how I liked, when I liked and didn't have to answer to anyone. Also I reflected on what I deserved and what I had achieved.

Most men in my position, alone on a tropical island, would have perished the first week, yet I not only survived but made friends along the way. Not for me alone in a cave tearing at raw flesh like a wild animal or skulking in the shadows living on berries and scraps left by others. I was my own person, not treading in the footsteps of others. I had killed a man, sent two others to their deaths, tried to save the life of another, killed a leopard and a baboon with my bare hands, watched my sweetheart die in my arms and saved the life of another woman. If that isn't enough to change one's thinking and outlook on life, I don't know what is.

*****

I had an austere upbringing in an orphanage, without the love and protection of a family home. Religious teaching was kept to a minimum, and moral issues tolerated provided you didn't ask too many questions. I've been interested in the environment and the world around us ever since I can remember, so it came as no surprise when I included them in my curriculum when I went to university. I was a bright lad, they said, and good at sports. Good at sports, maybe, and bright enough to scrape through with a B.Sc second, but not bright enough to see Heidi as she really was, but enough of that. The main thing was I was rid of her but maybe not in the way I would have chosen. It would be easy to blame Danny but the rot set in before he came along. She was bored from the word go; bored with the island and bored with me. Her life ended as mine began.

CHAPTER THIRTEEN

DEEP IN THE INTERIOR

Swirling veils of mist hung over the water and drifted upwards towards the canopy. Overhanging branches cut out the daylight. I could barely see were I was going, then the trees thinned out and it was daylight again.

I felt the first pangs of hunger, not having eaten for two days. I pulled into the side, secured the canoe and set off through the trees, threshing my way through some of the thickest jungle I had seen. I was rewarded with wildfowl, what else? It would seem Providence had laid by a plentiful supply especially for me. It would help, I thought, if they came stuffed and ready for the oven.

The difficulty was finding enough dry wood to make a fire. Matches get wet, that's why I carried a tinder-box. Preparing wildfowl for cooking and grilling it over an open fire had become second nature. As always the aroma attracted the usual onlookers, mostly monkeys whose petulance and childlike curiosity emboldened them to throw caution to the wind and come so close I could reach out and touch them.

*****

Off again, I followed the river mile after mile, stopping only when I was exhausted and could paddle no further. I covered sixty miles the first week, travelling faster than I did the first time. I had nowhere to go then. I did now.

I spotted the flickering fire and huddled figures I

had seen before. It was dark but it would always be dark here. It was that kind of place, cramped, shadowy, no daylight to relieve the gloom. Curiosity got the better of me. I secured the canoe and crept noiselessly through the undergrowth.

The half-darkness served me well. I could see without being seen. I almost cried out as I passed the most fiendishly protracted enactment of agonising, cold-blooded murder as ever devised by nature; a strangling fig tree, which, having encased its host tree in a vice-like grip, was slowly squeezing the life out of it until finally the host tree would be a living coffin and death a welcome relief. I had read about it, seen pictures of it but never in my wildest dreams thought I would witness it first-hand.

Next I came across a huge block of granite surrounded by a strip of rock, and at the outer edge a shelf of marble that reflected iridescently in the filtering sunlight, casting the same shimmering patterns as did the moon. There were no fire and huddling figures, after all. There was nothing only a trick of light and an optical illusion that fooled no one but myself.

*****

I returned to the canoe and clocked up the miles, consulting the map and compass as I went. Not knowing the course of the river and what pitfalls might befall me, I was prepared to travel the rest of the way on foot if necessary.

In my mind I tried to visualise what sort of woman Elizabeth was and why she decided to isolate herself from the world? Was it love or life itself? Irvie thought she was a born loner, capable of loving but distrusting its commitment, torturing herself with memories. The lines, 'I fell for your charms … And my arms held you tight,' seemed to reinforce this view. Such love was bound to hurt. There was no respite. Her only comfort was isolation, her only escape death.

*****

Passing along a calm stretch of water and letting the canoe drift along on its own, I was surprised to hear a cock crowing, but it was no farmyard bird; there were no farms for thousands of miles, and its call was a little different. Then I remembered that a cockerel's piercing cry is not designed to give townies something to moan about when they move to the country, but to penetrate the thick vegetation of rainforests. All chickens, domestic or otherwise, are descended from the oriental jungle fowl, but it still sounds startlingly incongruous to pass through a jungle and hear wild chickens crowing among the trees.

Rested, I picked up the paddles again and got into my usual rhythm, feeling a certain thrill, a wondrous sense of floating on air as I skimmed along swiftly and silently. I was making good time. I might even make it to the lagoon before nightfall. If I did I would make camp there. Not many people get the chance to spend the night in one of the most beautiful places on earth. I was happy, contented and at peace with the world. All that was missing was Cora.

*****

Two months had passed and I was spending most of my time paddling up rivers and negotiating bends, so I decided to abandon the canoe for a few days and see things as they were instead of endless travel stills as I passed by. Besides, I was getting cramp and needed to stretch my legs.

Another illusion befell me. It wasn't figures huddled around a fire this time, but a woman who might have been Cora who appeared from nowhere and ran in the opposite direction so fast I couldn't keep up with her. She had the smooth, fluent acceleration of an electric hare flirting with a greyhound. I was the greyhound. It was only when I lost sight of her and sat down that I wondered whether it was a figment of my imagination, after all, or Cora playing games? I knew why Heidi ran from me but what reason could Cora have? The same reason she had for disappearing, I suppose, whatever that may be. I didn't figure her the type to play games, but then I didn't figure on a lot of things. Illusion or not, it didn't stop me wanting to see her again.

Maybe I was being silly, maybe I was letting emotions cloud my judgement, maybe I was wrong. I'd been wrong before. Maybe I was reading into what wasn't there. It wouldn't be the first time. But my feelings were real enough. I had often thought how much happier I would be with Cora by my side accompanying me on my travels, make the cabin a real home, walking along holding hands laughing. Then it would be my Island of Dreams.

CHAPTER FOURTEEN

THE CAVES

I had never been as far north as this and saw nothing different except huge blocks of stone rising out of the ground which formed a circle not unlike the amphitheatre where the baboons lived, only there were no terraces, only caves.

Baboons lived here too. One came towards me, its head cocked on one side. I stood my ground. It was an old male, unsteady on his feet, tired and hungry. It had been banished from the troop to fend for itself and was not making a very good job of it. Too weak to reach the berries growing in crevices on the rock face, it was forced to scratch around for grubs and anything else it could find. It stood on all fours looking at me, much like a dog, even going back on its hind-legs in a begging position. I reached up as far as I could and not only pulled down enough berries for a good-sized meal but sufficient to last him a week. He ate quickly and greedily as if I might snatch them off back him.

"Take it easy, old boy," I murmured, "I'm not going to take it off you."

Suddenly he froze and rushed to my side, tugging at my sleeve, exhorting me to do something. I followed his gaze.

Three young males were approaching fast. Because I didn't run or do any of the usual things expected of me, they slowed down and, like the other baboons, were nervous and afraid. I smiled at the old boy to put him at ease, took hold of the machete I kept in a sheath slung across my back and walked towards them. I knew they wouldn't attack in numbers until one had taken me on single-handedly to prove himself, but, as before, I had no intention of participating in a ritual that meant nothing to me, but that didn't mean I was going to desert the old boy. They stopped. I went up close. They didn't know what to do at first and then tried to intimidate me by pulling faces and emitting low rasping growls but it didn't work, and then they made threatening gestures that didn't work either. I knew if I attacked first it would give them the impetus to retaliate and single combat would be forgotten. Not that I had any doubts about the outcome either way but I wanted to avoid bloodshed unless it was necessary. I was outnumbered but the machete redressed the balance.

I was deciding what to do when the old boy decided for me. He collapsed. I went over and gave him what comfort I could. It was touching the way he looked up at me before taking a deep breath and closing his eyes for the last time. I said a little prayer. When I got back to my feet the others had disappeared. Vultures appeared from nowhere but this was one meal they would have to go without. I covered the old boy's body with the biggest rocks I could find.

*****

I looked around. There were more caves than I gave credit for. One, the size of Earls Court ten times over, was breathtaking. I stepped inside, unaware of what I was getting myself into and found myself on a thick carpet of guano produced by millions of bats living in its roof. Wading back to the entrance was an unnerving experience since numerous low life scuttled across its surface, feeding on the guano and on each other. Nasty-looking insects with pincers, two centimetres long, fell from the roof and landed in my hair while others, appearing from nowhere, crawled up my legs.

Dusk was falling and to my horror the bats began to leave their perches in two and threes, their numbers increasing as they flew around windmill fashion to a cacophony of twittering cries. By the time I had left the cave and scraped the vile droppings from my boots, they were streaming over my head in their hundreds of thousands, wheeling vortexes snaking upwards before disappearing in the darkening sky.

*****

When I said this part of the island was no more exciting than the area I was used to, what I meant was I couldn't see myself living there. I had come through the worst the island could offer and marvelled at its best, even picking up a few friends on the way, but the cabin was my home. As for friends: The baboons were my friends. None matched them for affection and loyalty. Yet such sentiments were not necessarily extended to their own kind. The old boy for instance. They would have ostracised and treated him in exactly the same way. Their culture didn't allow for anyone who couldn't pull their weight, and, like it or not, the old boy was barely strong enough to eat, let alone do his bit to ensure the troop's survival, which means they were no better and no worse than the three young males I protected him from.

*****

With these thoughts running through my mind, I went back to the canoe and was on the move again, paddling northwards as far as I could before night set in, and made camp in a meadow where the intoxicating aroma of flowers and the gentle hum of the wind blowing through the trees lulled me to sleep.

I awoke the next morning to the twitter of birds of every colour of the rainbow hopping around as they fed off the lush grass, whilst in the morning sky two eagles were locked in a freefall gavotte as they competed for air space. Survival comes in many shapes and forms. I settled for a drink from the nearest river where a fish just happened to be passing.

*****

The weather was hazy for the next couple of days. The canoe tossed and turned as the river surged through a narrow channel before settling down again, by which time I had lost all sense of direction and could only guess at the route I was taking since the compass was wet and might give a wrong reading. The map was better. Symbols took me every inch of the way. The caves, appropriately representing by the letter C, were sixty miles from my destination. Seeing that I had come ten miles since then, it was perfectly reasonable to assume I was now fifty miles from my destination. The journey had been long and tiring. At times I wondered if it was ever going to end.

I was of sound mind and limb except for a nagging feeling that I wasn't alone. I could swear I heard someone cry out. I looked about me. No one was there. It was all I could do to convince myself that I wasn't losing my marbles.

Hallucinations were becoming more frequent. The

girl running through the trees was the first and wouldn't be the last. Perhaps I was losing my marbles, after all, or hadn't adjusted to the jungle as well as I thought. Or perhaps subconsciously I was longing to go home. But this was my home. All that was missing was Cora, and when I found her I could settle down. I felt drowsy. Perhaps the journey had taken more out of me than I cared to admit.

CHAPTER FIFTEEN

JOURNEY'S END

As I approached Elizabeth's encampment a great sadness overtook me. The very thought of being alone here with limited resources, whether there were native boys to lend a hand or not, made me wonder why Elizabeth went there in the first place.

In this vast wilderness, with death snapping at your heels, it would be difficult for anyone to live something approaching a normal life, let alone a woman in her fifties. I could at least get around and make friends, even if they were not the kind you would take home to meet mother. Elizabeth had her memories, but even they can be unpleasant sometimes.

On reflection, perhaps she wasn't as miserable as it would seem; martyring away with a broken heart while the rest of the world turns the other way. I'm inclined to think she became a recluse for fear of being hurt or consideration for those who might get hurt. She could have persuaded Irvie to leave his wife if she had really wanted to. Instead she was off on her travels before he could make up his mind. If love means being happy making someone else happy, then she was in love.

*****

I nosed around. Although the jungle had reclaimed most of the clearing, I could seed traces of its original outline. All that was left of the lean-to where Elizabeth lived were a few tattered strips of canvas, a hammock worse for wear and pots and pans hanging over a makeshift draining-board and a few books and things exactly as she had left them. Enamel jugs and basins provided lodgings for a variety of bugs and beetles.

I flicked through the books, yellow with age but still readable. One caught my eye: Alice In Wonderland. I turned to the page where the White Rabbit recites the verse to the King of Hearts. I smiled, put the book down and rummaged through the rest of the stuff. There were no souvenirs, photographs, nothing, as if she cancelled out the past and kept her fingers crossed for the future.

I felt like a peeping Tom until I remembered who I was and why I was there, then felt personally involved and knew Elizabeth hadn't died in vain. That I hadn't been forgotten was borne out when I spotted 'Little Kieron' on a book mark, scribbled perhaps when she was reflecting on what might have been

I heard the cry again and ignored it, having more important things on my mind like finding Elizabeth's grave. I could imagine it occupying a place of reverence, elaborate but not overdone, in the shade and out of the glare of the sun where visitors might pay their respect in comfort. As it turned out I couldn't have painted a more accurate picture. It was on the fringe of the encampment where it was coolest, where the soothing purl of a stream and gentle whisper of the breeze lent dignity and gravitas. A headstone, hewn out of marble, bore the inscription:

Elizabeth Monica Argyll,
Born 9th December 1925.
Died 2nd March 1975.
REST IN PEACE

I gathered two bunches of wild orchids, put them in a couple of pots lying around, watered them from the brook and stood them at the foot of the headstone. The surround was covered with fine grass and flowers as if regularly attended, but I knew different. To my knowledge there was no one else on the island except Cora and me. But then, there might only be me. A leopard might have had her or a thousand other things might have happened. I shuddered at the thought. I heard the cry again. It came over loud and clear. I put it down to an over-active imagination.

It is true that solemn occasions begat solemn thoughts but not for me they didn't. I was relieved, if anything, that visiting Elizabeth's grave wasn't as traumatic as it might have been, given that it should have been my first priority. As it was, my first priority was staying alive.

*****

I spent the rest of the day pottering around, putting things in their place and tidying up as if expecting Elizabeth to show up. But she never would. She was where she wanted to be. I recalled the diaries: 'His pain is my pain, his happiness my happiness.' In my mind I could hear her laughing as she pretended to stumble and smile when Irvie held her in his arms. I hoped she was smiling down on me. Providence had brought me here. I hoped the same would guide me safely away.

I decided to stay the night, not out of respect to her memory for I had never met her, or, should I say I was too young to recall being handed over to the authorities, but I didn't hold that against her. She was a victim of the wrong time and the wrong place. I was satisfied just being there, to stand where she had stood, walk where she had walked and sleep where she had slept.

*****

The next morning I had a strip wash in the stream and breakfasted on black mangoes, disgusting to look at but nice to eat, and then toured the place in case I had missed something. I wasn't being nosey, just curious, that's all. Elizabeth had been wise to make this her home. I would have made it my home too but I had my cabin and friends to go back to.

Apart from the cries and other tricks of my imagination, it couldn't have worked out better. I compared myself with others, and thanked the grace of God for giving me the health and strength to achieve what I had set out to do, yet I knew I was far from finished. Sometimes it is easier to arrive than depart, and I didn't need to be told there would be many more pitfalls and close shaves before I got back to my cabin. I would visit Newtown first, of course, at the same time keeping an eye out for Cora. If she were still on the island, I would find her. If not, so be it.

Although it seemed only yesterday when she disappeared, my image of her had transformed into something akin to what I would have liked her to be other than what she was: Not a child of nature but a child of my dreams; coquettish, seductive with a penchant for appearing and leaving without trace. Imagination again? It seemed I was doing nothing else than mould images to suit my fancies in spite of no one knew better than me that eschewing reality in favour of fantasy would be a mistake I would pay for with my life.

*****

I had visited Elizabeth's grave and that should have been it but I hung around for the next couple of days doing nothing except eating and sleeping, neither of which I indulged with my usual enthusiasm. I kept asking myself if I was in love with Cora, and if so was it in the same way Elizabeth had been in love with Irvie? Both had been consummated, only in Cora's case it may have been done out of gratitude. I always read into some thing that wasn't there anyway. One could say I fell in love too easy. Maybe so but there was no denying that Cora was the type of girl with whom any man would find it impossible not to fall in love. She had probably forgotten me by now. Given time I would forget her, it's just that I have a longer memory, that's all.

I was a born romantic and there was nothing I could do about except perhaps adopt an attitude alien to my nature and see things as they were instead of as I wanted them to be. I'm sure that if Cora had read my thoughts she would have laughed her head off. We had met once and she went as suddenly as she came. Perhaps that is why she did leave. She didn't want a scene. Let's face it, what love there was resided in my mind.

I visited the grave again, said a little prayer and was on my way. The cry that began to haunt me haunted me again, plaintive, calling for help. I ignored it. The compass was still wet so I took my bearings from the map. I was smack on course. Newtown was on the coast where the river poured into the ocean, so it was back to the sea again.

*****

The canoe glided over the water as I paddled with renewed vigour. I didn't have far to go, ten miles at the most. This part of the rainforest was no different from the rest, the same old hazards, the same old mishaps. The river was particularly turbulent at one point, threatening to capsize me. I saw my first buffalo. It looked up as I passed, gave me a cursory glance and carried on grazing. I'm sure I heard a helicopter. I looked up and all I could see were trees.

CHAPTER SIXTEEN

NEWTOWN AND OTHER ADVENTURES

I didn't know what to expect when I got to Newtown. All I know is it couldn't have been further from what I imagined it would be. A collection of log cabins sums it up, with a Spanish-style house built of wood that would be where the Commissioner lived, a privy tucked discreetly out of the way and the tattered remains of a tarpaulin flapping in the breeze on wooden uprights that would have been where the stores were kept. I had read about ghost towns but never thought I would find myself in one. Still, there's a first time for everything and I'd had enough 'first times' since coming to the island to last a lifetime, and knew there would be more.

I walked to the water's edge and stood looking out over the Pacific Ocean, and the reef inshore that was almost at my feet. There is a popular misconception that the coral reef is the work of an insect; an insect revered as the paragon of industry and hard work. Nothing could be further from the truth. Given to a life of ease and degeneracy, it uses elements from the water to make itself a home and lets someone else do the building – the water itself, and when it dies leaves behind a legacy of industry undeserved and completely untrue. On a reef you are looking at the so-called work of the polypifers, as the insects are called, that over the years have in fact left behind evidence of their moronic and rather useless lives. It is also commonly believed that the reef is formed of dead rocks when in fact it is alive. If it were not it would not be able to resist the action of the sea over the years. Always dying, always recovering, devoured by fish, ravaged by the sea, the life of a coral reef is not a bed of roses. It is as alive as a plant or a tree. Every storm, every ocean wave tears a piece off which the living coral replaces.

The screams of seabirds rang in my ears as they circled over the chopping waves and dived beneath the surface. The boiling hot sun hung in the sky like a ball of fire. I pulled my hat forward to shield my eyes. Sweat poured off me. I wiped my neck and face with clumps of grass.

I spotted a ship too far away to determine whether it was coming or going, and the helicopter I thought I heard. I lapsed into thought, and when I looked again the helicopter had disappeared and the ship was a speck on the horizon.

It said a lot for my peace of mind that, considering the time I had spent on the island and all I had been through, neither the ship nor the helicopter evoked memories that made me wish I was on either taking it easy watching the world go by. Civilisation and all it stood for meant nothing to me.

*****

A landing stage caught my eye. New spars replaced ones that were worn and broken, and other bits and pieces had been added. It reached out over the reef where the water was deep enough to accommodate craft that otherwise wouldn't be able to offload their cargo. A jib to facilitate offloading stood idle collecting rust over the years, but not so the landing stage where evidence of recent activity was plain to see; grass trodden into the ground by many feet, bushes brushed to one side where people had passed and other tell-tale signs. Also there was a circle of flattened grass not unlike a crop circle.

If there was a motorboat there had to be a place to house it. It wasn't hard to find, not far from where I moored the canoe. It was a brick structure, solid, well built and impossible to break into without a stick of dynamite.

Next I looked in the cabins. They were pokey little holes, with the bare necessities, each with a paraffin lamp similar to the ones in my cabin, and the most primitive shower baths I had seen. The house, in contrast – door lock conveniently broken - was furnished in the modern style, with all the mod cons including a pool table and a well-stocked bar. Baroque fireplaces and marble surrounds gave the place atmosphere. All in all the abode of a family with no money problems, who could come and go as they please. An outside generator provided the electricity and pumped water from a well. It was housed in a brick surround with ventilator grills next to the cupboard where the fuel was kept.

*****

For some reason I had a fear of being attacked during the night, something that had never troubled me before, and I was almost paranoiac in ensuring my safety, choosing a cabin to sleep in instead of the house where burglars were more likely to practise their skills. The odds against meeting a burglar on a South Sea island never occurred to me. Like the hallucinations, it was another mental aberration, the price I paid for treading the unknown and battling with inner demons.

I hung around for a couple of days waiting for the occupants to return. I took nothing from the house because there was nothing I wanted. I got my own food and anything else I required.

I toured the house again looking for something that would tell me what kind of people lived there. Cora sprang to mind but we met deep in the interior and she looked no more tired than if she had been for a stroll in the local park, let alone trek for months through rainforests. She might know her way around but she wasn't that fast unless she came by motorboat. The rivers, criss-crossing the island like motorways, were handy for getting from one place to another.

*****

There were two rooms downstairs and three upstairs not counting a bathroom. I had almost forgotten what a bathroom looked like. I was tempted to tale advantage of it and freshen up but knew if I did I would be no better than a common housebreaker, a thief who takes what he can like a rat scavenging in dustbins when no one's around. There was nothing stopping me looking though. There were talcum powder, deodorants, toothpaste, half a dozen aerosols, soap and after-shave etc. I liked the smell of soap but couldn't stand after-shave. I sprayed perfume in the air. It reminded me of Heidi. She bought it by the gallon and I was sick of it but this time was different. I could walk away.

For the first time I noticed how stuffy it was and was tempted to open the windows but didn't want the occupants to know they'd had visitors. I left everything as I found it and checked the cabins again.

I was drawn to one in particular. Particles of dust

danced in the sunlight through the window that cast shadows on the walls. I felt a sudden chill. At my feet was a sprig of heather. I examined it. It was fresh as if it had been picked that morning. Although no one was there, I knew I wasn't alone.

*****

I went for a stroll on the seashore. Thousands of crabs had the beach to themselves. I hadn't gone far when the sweep of the shoreline revealed a brooding, steaming wilderness where towering cliffs jutted out to sea. They were part of a mountain range that created an enclave entirely cut off from the rest of the island. Turtles and seals basked and lazed in its shadows, while inshore flycatchers and humming birds made nests in towering sandalwood trees, a picture fit for any calendar.

The enclave was depicted on the map in blue pencil and occupied a large slice of the northwest. After thousands of years, chances are it had its own treasure of wildlife evolved to suit the peculiarities of its environment.

*****

As I walked black clouds blocked out the sun and the calm sea turned into a lashing, unrelenting ocean. Mountainous waves came thundering inshore carrying with it a black and white murderous presence. The turtles and seals didn't know what hit them. As the crests of the waves turned back on themselves and disappeared under the weight of new ones, black and white flanks rode the waves towards the shore and surged up the beach in a maelstrom of threshing and high-pitched squeals. As the turtles and seals scattered in alarm, a seal was tossed high in the air, and no sooner had it splashed back into the water than it was tossed again. This went on half a dozen times until the seal was dead, seized in powerful jaws and then swallowed. Then the sun came out from behind the clouds and the sea was as calm as before. The turtles and seals carried on basking and lazing as if nothing had happened. The killer whale doesn't waste time.

The fun wasn't over. I was heading back the way I came when suddenly the sea lions and turtles made a sudden dash for the sea as if they hadn't had enough trauma already. I didn't have to look twice to see why. A bull, the embodiment of mayhem and destruction, was heading my way challenging everything that stood in its way. My only escape was the escarpment. There was a ledge ten metres up where I could sit it out until the bull grew tired and went back the way he came.

*****

A cleft, home to shrubs and small trees, cut deep into the escarpment from top to bottom, with insets where terns and guillemots nested. I began to climb. In normal circumstances I would take the bull on, but this was open country with nowhere to hide, nothing to confuse and counter its superior size and strength. To engage it head on would be sheer madness. It snorted and pawed the ground as if it knew what I was thinking. It took me two hours to reach the ledge that cut deep into the rock. I looked down. The bull was nowhere to be seen, a ridge of low-lying hills were visible in the distance.

I must have dozed off because the next thing I knew it was morning and I waking up to fresh mountain air and the cries of vultures circling above me. They lost interest when I sat up.

At first I wondered where I was, then my head cleared. I thought that, having come this far, I might as well go the whole hog and take a look at the enclave if only to see what it looked like, if I didn't run out of ledge. I didn't. I was lucky. The ledge went as far as I wanted it to and I found myself looking out over what probably nobody else had ever laid eyes since time began. A lost world, untrammelled, untouched by human hand. Climbing down was easier than climbing up. Thick clumps of vine helped me on my way.

*****

The terrain was new to me, some of the animals unlike anything I had seen. Their glares said the same about me. Leopards were familiar but no friends of mine. The first law of the jungle is knowing your enemy. I kept my distance.

After a couple of hours, I decided to go back the way I came but it wasn't as simple as that. Vines are easier for climbing down than up, as I found out when I fell and almost dislocated my shoulder. I could see no other way back to the ledge. I went for a walk before trying again.

I came across a pool in a forest clearing and joined bush pig and roebuck to slake my thirst. All was peace and quiet until a sixth sense told me we weren't alone. I froze. The roebuck did the same. Out of the corner of my eye I saw a sleek body in the long grass. Longer and lighter than the leopard, it resembled the cheetah without the tear marks. The bush pig grunted and carried on drinking while the deer jostled in fear and panic.

Suddenly it erupted into view, its gaze locked on a yearling calf that had strayed from the herd. Within seconds it reached sixty miles per hour, its supple body extending to lengthen its stride until it was almost airborne. The jinking calf aspired to prodigious manoeuvres in order to hang on to dear life. It was losing ground when a twist of fate levelled the odds. Surging forward to hug the erratic curve of its zig-zagging prey, the cat made a final leap that would have spelt death to the calf had it not leaned over too far and fell on its knees. The cat, carried on by its own momentum, finished up on its back pawing the air, all wind knocked out of it. The calf quickly rejoined the herd and we all carried on drinking as if nothing had happened. The cat limped away to regain both strength and dignity. I had never seen such speed.

*****

I was on my way back to take another crack at the ledge when I spotted open country through the trees that had escaped my notice earlier. It was out of my way but a quick peek wouldn't hurt anybody.

A shimmering plain of pastoral beauty stretched before me, with trees dotted here and there and flowers of a thousand hues making exquisite mosaic. A herd of deer disappeared in a sea of bobbing tails behind a trellis of hibiscus, butterflies gathered in swarms and a lone bull grazed in the distance. It was sheer heaven. But then, everything about the island was heaven except the cruelty perpetrated by the hunter on the hunted that is necessary so that others may live.

It was as if I ceased to exist. I saw no one and no one saw me. Months of paddling up rivers and trekking through rainforests had instilled in me the need for company yet content to be alone. Solitude is all very well, but when you walk the unknown you walk alone. Also it plays tricks with the imagination: Cora running through the trees, for example; a feeling of being followed when nobody's there; a sense of being alone when someone's with you, and the cries, plaintive melancholy, haunting, mocking. The figures huddled around the fire were explained by a trick of light. I wished everything could be explained so easily. But then wouldn't life be boring?

CHAPTER SEVENTEEN

GREEN FIRE

Returning to the cliff, I scoured the escarpment for a way back up to the ledge when I came across a huge mound of earth and uprooted trees where there had been a landslide. I gave it no more than a cursory glance when crystals twinkling like green fire in the mouth of a cave that had been crushed by a huge rock caught my eye.

It took me an hour to fight my way through the debris. The caves walls had collapsed and were literally turned inside out, and what I saw took my breath away. It was a veritable Aladdin's cave; schistose rock in which emerald crystals coruscated in glittering brilliance.

I dug some out with the axe, swinging it feverishly for fear I was hallucinating again and they would disappear. I examined them. It was emerald, pure and simple, not brillium the emerald's equivalent of fool's gold, but emerald, one hundred per cent emerald. I couldn't believe my eyes. They ranged from small, handsome crystals of a pale hue to ones showing mossiness due to tiny air bubbles and fissures.

Perfect crystals are hard to come by but if there were more seams of schistose rock in the mountains, and I didn't see why there shouldn't be, the chances of finding them were very good indeed. I ran what I had through my fingers like some grasping miser, counting them again and again. I made it three hundred and twenty.

Like a gold prospector stricken with gold fever, I dug out more making a grand total of three hundred and thirty. Too bulky to carry and not relishing the prospect of humping them by other means, I stuffed some in my pocket and left the rest where they were. Of course, I didn't take them for financial reasons. Where would I convert them into cash, and, if I could, what would I buy? I simply took them as ornaments for my cabin, something to put on the shelf that didn't previously belong to someone else. Not that I wanted to show them off to visitors. I didn't get any visitors, only the baboons and they couldn't care less.

*****

It took a while for the full implications of it to sink in. Not many people discover an emerald mine in a land time forgot. The thing is I must keep a sense of proportion and not let my thoughts stray from my resolve to renounce the life I had left behind. If I did stray, everything I had achieved, the happiness and tears, would be lost.

Having riches beyond the dreams of avarice is hard to grasp. I could buy a castle in Spain, with flunkeys everywhere and friends who were not friends, but would I be happy? Wouldn't I miss my real friends the baboons, and the magic of sitting under a tropical moon by the fire listening to nocturnal birdsong and other sounds of the forest?

Truth is, I had everything I wanted. All that was missing was Cora. Yet there was a downside. What if she yielded to the very temptations I resisted when she learned what I had found, if she wasn't wealthy herself, that is? Or if she was wealthy, would she give up life's luxuries to be with me? She might not even like me. But I did make her laugh. Surely that meant something.

It is a defect inseparable from the way of life that the good things are not so good when they can no longer be of use, and that no matter what we give to others we keep sufficient for ourselves. There isn't a man in the universe who wouldn't envy my position; money to burn, everything I desire at my finger-tips. But what did it amount to? That I could outbid others? Have what they didn't have? But, if like the proverbial miser, I kept my wealth under lock and key and didn't let it be known that I had more than my neighbours, no one would be any the wiser and I would be accepted as one of them. My point being that if I didn't mention the emeralds, no one would profit, there would be no losers, I would be left alone and life would go on as usual.

*****

The day wore on. I didn't realise the time until the sun went down. It was only when I heard the cry of the gulls and the waves licking the shoreline that I remembered I wasn't far from the sea. I gathered fruit and set about making shelter for the night among the debris, collecting as many branches as I could, shaking them free of termites and other creatures, before spreading them out like a bed.

Sleep didn't come easy. I tossed and turned, plagued by dreams and nightmares. When I was finally settled for the night the baying of wild dogs awoke me again.

I scrambled around desperately in the moonlight gathering as many leaves as I could find, attached them to lengths of vines and strung them around my 'bed' like Christmas decorations so that when the wind blew they fluttered like birds' wings. About fifty per cent of canines that live in the wild, except the fox, are nervous of movements emulating flapping wings and will turn back rather than find out what's making it, yet have no compunction about attacking birds themselves. European wolf-hunters regularly use this method for laying traps using string and newspaper.

I slept with one eye open and the machete in my hand. The dogs either went in another direction or confirmed the fluttering method worked because I didn't hear them again.

*****

The next morning I had another crack at the escarpment. The ledge was proving to be a nuisance as if it knew what I was trying to do and was laughing at me. On the other side were footholds and ledges to hang on to, whereas this side was sheer rock face except for a few shrubs here and there. As before, the thick clumps of vine didn't help any. I would just have to start climbing and hope for the best.

At the third attempt I managed to reach a corridor of roots that spiralled upwards and at one point passed over the sea. I clung to the roots for dear life, aching all over, not daring to look down. Not that it made any difference. The breakers pounding the cliffs told me what would happen if I fell. I wasn't as agile as I thought I was, but I was determined and had strong arms and legs. I gripped each root firmly before letting go of the other. Slowly but surely I was getting there, then, horror of horrors, I lost my footing and fell.

I remember a splash, that's all. I was numb and confused and the next thing I knew I was treading water. I swam as best I could when the underflow sucked me under, and my lungs almost burst as I fought to get back to the surface. Then a towering wave engulfed me and carried me out to sea. I swam for all I was worth struggling to keep my head above water. Then down I went again, and when I resurfaced I was tossed high in the air, and so it went on, flailing, dipping, rising, then I couldn't believe my luck. The sea settled down and I was deposited safely on the shore as if nothing had happened. I lay down exhausted and dried out.

Throughout all this the machete slung across my back was no encumbrance. I didn't even know it was there.

I had another stroke of luck. A herd of buffalo passed within yards off me and disappeared in the foliage at the foot of a mountain. I followed. A fissure sliced the mountain in half forming a tunnel to the other side. Daylight from above cast eerie shadows on the damp uneven walls. The buffalo moved in single file, their bulk not detracting from their sure-footedness acquired over centuries traversing the same route. They knew the way blindfold. Like elephants, the matriarch was in front, and like elephants, they ventured where no other animal dare go. The young were in the middle and the young bulls brought up the rear. More than once they turned in my direction as a warning not to get too close. At one point the tunnel widened into a chamber carpeted with familiar bat droppings. There was a flurry of movement and winged shadows disappeared into the gloom like phantoms of the night. Not unfamiliar either. The buffalo pressed on unconcerned. The ones behind gave the little ones a reassuring nudge to keep them moving. The matriarch was a hard pacemaker.

*****

At last we emerged into the bright sunshine. Before

me was no longer the brooding, steaming wilderness I saw before but a gateway to freedom. Not that the enclave was anything like a prison but I felt trapped all the same.

I went one way and the buffalo went another. It was a leisurely stroll returning to Newtown as I looked out over the ocean. I sang with the gulls and breathed the sea air, and considered myself lucky to be alive. I had taken risks, even cheated death and would go on cheating death until I settled down, and I couldn't see that happening for a long time.

It was with some disquiet that I noticed I had developed the habit of talking to myself, not for reasons of insanity brought on my solitary existence, but because perhaps subconsciously I feared losing the gift of speech through lack of practice as I've heard happens to people who lead a lifestyle similar to my own.

*****

I couldn't wait to get back home. I missed my friends the baboons, the familiar haunts and the beach where it all began. Things were different then. I was different, my whole life was different. I was not so susceptible to the wiles and guiles of women as I once was in spite of being drawn to Cora, whom, I hasten to add, was no ordinary woman. I learnt more about women in the short space of time I had been with her than in the whole of my life previously.

With these thoughts running through my mind I fell into a leisurely pace and was getting along nicely when it started to rain. There was no warning. It didn't start as a drizzle and finish up as a downpour. It started as a downpour and finished up as a downpour. There was no in between. It lasted five hours. I took shelter in a copse of bushes, which restricted freedom of movement but kept me dry.

A herd of inquisitive feral cattle greeted me as I crawled back out into the daylight. I wasn't a pretty sight, stiff all over and crawling with slugs and ticks and things. The cattle carried on grazing. I freshened up as best I could in the first watering hole I came to.

CHAPTER EIGHTEEN

ON MY WAY HOME

At the rear of the Commissionaire's house was a sight that would have surprised anyone except me. I ran out of surprises long ago. Inside an enclosure surrounded by a wire fence were a neatly clipped lawn, tennis court, swimming pool, deck chairs, sun lounges, tables, chairs and other paraphernalia of the privileged and the wealthy. But how did the privileged and wealthy get there in the first place? The helicopters came to mind. I had seen two and heard one, which makes three or the same one each time. And to think I mistook this place for a ghost town. The adage that life is full of surprises might have been coined where I stood. From the 'lost world' to a resort that wouldn't look out of place on the Riveria certainly takes some believing. I would have considered myself a lucky man if I didn't belief there is no such thing as a free lunch. There is always a price to pay. I was on my guard.

I did another tour of the house. I realised for the first time how expensive the furnishings were. Each room was carpeted in thick pile and each room beautifully furnished, with abstract paintings on every wall including the bathroom, which reminded me it would do no harm if I took a bath after all. I certainly needed one, what with following the buffalo thorough the mountains and sheltering from the rain in the bushes. l would leave the place exactly as I found it and no one would be any the wiser. Watering holes have their uses but substituting for a bath isn't one of them.

One look at the bathroom decided me against it. It was pristine clean and would be a sacrilege for the likes of me, weathered and gnarled, to take advantage of what it had to offer without saying the Lord's Prayer and three Hail Marys afterwards. I would take a dip in the pool instead. While I was about it I would wash my clothes. No one would know.

I stripped off and washed my trousers and things in the sink and then laid them out to dry by the side of the pool along with the emeralds, machete, knife and axe, and dived in. I've no idea how many times I swam up and down. I lost track of time. I must have been an awesome sight, like some latter-day Tarzan or the wild man of Borneo doing as I pleased and taking what I fancied. But it wasn't like that. I took nothing I wouldn't have been given had the occupants been at home.

After about an hour I climbed out, lay on the grass under the burning sun, closed my eyes and fell asleep.

In my dream they were running over the heather. She fell, he picked her up and held her in his arms.

Only it wasn't Elizabeth and Irvie, it was Cora and me. I don't know how long I was asleep, half-hour, hour maybe. Either I was very tired or it was because it was the first time I had really relaxed since leaving the cabin, 'relaxed' being the operative word. No one knew more than I did that in the jungle where each sound is a warning and each movement a threat, relax is the last thing you do.

Millionaire's playground or not, it was still the jungle and I was as vulnerable to attacks from leopards and other sundry creatures that might be inquisitive and didn't know their own strength as I would ever be. A tree is different, you can see above as well as below. Even palm leaves and bamboo offer some protection, but spread out on a lawn as naked as the day you were born on an island teeming with wild animals is asking for trouble.

The fence was no protection. I was thinking it was no more use than an ornament when a terminal caught my eye. Of course, it was an electric fence. I should have known. No one leaves stuff like this out in the open without taking measures to ensure it remains there even on an island where the chances of it being stolen are so rare as to be negligible. The house was wired up as well but presumably short-circuited when the lock was broken. My clothes were dry. I put them on.

A bear, not unlike the sloth bear, bigger, more upright, peered quizzically through the fence. Like most animals, bears are not dangerous unless provoked. The electric wire might just do the trick, frighten it without making it angry, but it padded away without touching it and I didn't see it again.

*****

Up to then I had been quite content, sleeping, eating, hunting, exploring, always on the move. But now a spirit of restlessness came over me. I wanted to go someplace else, do something different but, of course, that was silly. It may have been civilisation crying out to me, the cities, the streets, the cars, the vices and other temptations; the whole maelstrom of modern life, the smells, the grime and everything else it stands for. But that could never be. This was my home, and I knew if I gave in to these little whims it was unlikely I would be in a position to return and I would regret it for the rest of my life.

It was the first time I had enjoyed such opulence; swimming pool, posh house, posh furniture, the whole bag of tricks. Cora sprang to mind. Was she the reason for my unrest? Perhaps I was thinking of her more than I should. If she placed no importance on the time we spent together, I was a fool. If she had completely forgotten me, I was a bigger fool.

*****

Letting myself back into the house, I was drawn to the kitchen. In spite of my resolve not to take anything that didn't belong to me, I did, however, bite into a carrot from the vegetable rack as I had forgotten what carrots tasted like, as well as potatoes, cabbages, turnips, parsnips, swedes, peas, onions and other vegetables.

It was nice to eat but would have been nicer cooked. Vegetables were the one thing I hadn't included on my list of essentials that would make my Island of Dreams more like home, but where do I get them? I was no gardener but I knew how to plant seeds and make them grow.

*****

I had secured the canoe well away from the estuary but the incoming tide still rocked it violently. I untied it with one hand and held with the other so it wouldn't be snatched from my grasp. I looked forward to visiting Elizabeth's grave again on my way home. I would change the flowers for fresh ones.

I was soon paddling away as usual, battling with turbulent undertows and dodging overhanging branches. At one point swarms of butterflies gathered on a grass bank. Some had settled and some hovered a couple of inches above the ground. I steadied the canoe and watched. The ones above join the ones below until they resembled clusters of flowers. It was their protection against being eaten by birds. Ironically, the camouflage was so effective it fooled everyone including bees who thought they were real flowers and attacked them anyway looking for nectar.

*****

Further downstream I put ashore to take in the scenery. I picked the wrong spot. The vegetation ran riot. All manner of roots and ankle-twisting plants made walking difficult, and where they left off bogs and mires took their place. I stopped to wipe the sweat off my face when stalks and stems sprang back up from nowhere and wrapped around my legs like tentacles. I hacked and pulled to break free.

The air was damp and sticky, and the perpetual buzz of insects harmonised with other choruses that went on twenty-fours hours a day. A bulldozer making inroads into this labyrinth of clutching, grasping, ankle-breaking plant life today, would find little evidence it had ever been there six months later. I got back into the canoe.

*****

The dream came back to me, as did the hallucinations and voices. My circumstances, such as they were, suited me fine and appealed to my nature, and I could see no reason for these chimeras unless my preoccupation with Cora was greater than I thought. It was ironic that the qualities that drew me to her made nonsense of my resolve to keep women at arm's length.

I asked myself time and time again whether I would ever meet her again, even questioned my own credibility as to whether I had met her in the first place. I had met her, no doubt about that, and if I was lucky I would meet her again.

CHAPTER NINETEEN

I PRAY FOR THE FIRST TIME

I knelt at the side of Elizabeth's grave. Nothing had changed; the soothing purl of the stream, the gentle whisper of the breeze, the orchids I had put in the pots.

For the first time I prayed. I remembered a couple of prayers from childhood and repeated them over and over again, even if I didn't fully grasp their meaning and had not yet come to terms with Elizabeth being my mother. I had never thought of her that way. She was a goal, a destination, something I had to achieve; something I owed to a dying man who said he was my father, who wanted me to put flowers on a grave, the grave of someone I had never met, someone who gave life, a life that owed me nothing beyond what I put into it, a life with its ups and down, laughter and tears.

It was then I took stock of myself. I was far from perfect and thanked Providence for being alive. That I had been on the island for almost a year and not sustained any serious injury said a lot for my good fortune. I had done no more than your average man would do in similar circumstances except, perhaps, I was more direct in my approach whereas your average man would have wilted and paid for it with his life.

*****

The last time I was at Elizabeth's encampment I stayed the night and saw no point in breaking the habit. It rained all day. I sheltered in the trees. I felt a headache coming on. I passed it off as nothing until it got unbearable then I made myself a den by bending the branches of a sapling, securing them to the ground and covering them over with palm leaves. I crawled inside as one crawls into a tunnel. It was no different from the copse of bushes where I sheltered the last time, cramped, dry and full of slugs and ticks and things.

I lay in the darkness for hours, shivering and sweating in the throes of a fever. The pain got worse and I thought my head would burst. If that wasn't enough, I had another dream, this time about Heidi.

It didn't make sense. First Cora and now Heidi. I had forgotten Heidi unless she lingered in my subconscious as a contrast between good and evil, warning me not to make the same mistake twice.

*****

The rain didn't let up, destroying what it could and battering and bending what it couldn't. My biggest fear was it turning into a hurricane and then I would be in trouble. I couldn't move, every joint ached, I couldn't even get comfortable. I lost track of time. At one stage I almost cried out, the pain was so bad, then, after hours that never seemed to end, the fever lifted and I was my old self again. Weak perhaps, but it could have been worse.

Dusk was falling. I went hunting for game to build up my strength. I had left my knife in the tunnel so was forced to kill with my bare hands, not a pleasant prospect at the best of times. I spotted half a dozen wildfowl, what else, who ran in different directions when they saw me, squawking and flapping their wings? I went for the slowest. It gave me a run for my money until it ran bang smack into a tree and knocked itself out. I dispatched it as quickly as I could.

Fortunately, the tinder-box was dry so making a fire was not difficult. There was plenty of dry wood if you knew where to look, preferably on the underside of branches of the bigger trees; twigs so dry and brittle you could snap them with your fingers. In no time I was eating roast wildfowl and bedded down for the night in the den but not before making it comfortable, and had my first good night's sleep in what seemed like years.

*****

Next morning I went to collect the canoe. I had moored it on a low shoreline clear of the water. Now it was high water and the canoe was waterlogged due to the rain. Fortunately, it was made out of balsa wood and as light as a feather, so it wasn't difficult to turn it upside down and get it back into working order.

*****

I had paid my respects to Elizabeth and was on my way. To anyone else it would seem a waste of time. Not for me it wasn't. It was a privilege and experience I'm not likely to forget. Hadn't I learnt because of her how to survive in the jungle on wit and strength alone? Not for me ropes, tents, water purifier, hunting rifle, traps, pills to ward off malaria, anti-sunburn cream and the rest of the paraphernalia. I was a one-man survival team, self-taught with a leopard and baboon to my credit. Not that it's anything to brag about. I killed them because I had to. It was either them or me. I didn't like it any more than they did.

*****

Weeks passed and I followed the same route as before. Some scenes I remembered, others slipped from my mind. I felt as if I had conquered the world as the canoe skimmed along. If not conquered, I was one of the richest men in it. I stopped to examine the emeralds, running them through my fingers.

I did have my reservations, however, about leaving the others behind. What if someone stole them? The fact that there were probably mountains of the stuff and the chances of anyone finding a way into the enclave were a million to one escaped me. Even if the island was teeming with people, who would think of going under the mountains as the buffalo did? It was because of them that I got out. Besides, there was no one on the island except Cora, me, and the people who used the Commissionaire's house as a holiday home, who probably had enough emeralds of their own anyway. Either way, no one would be foolish enough to venture into the enclave as I did, let alone find a way out. I was the only one who knew my way around.

When I said I took the same route as before, I didn't mean I did it through choice. It was force of habit, which I broke by taking another route along a tributary that I was to regret. A cavernous mouth and gaping teeth broke the surface of the water in one mad swirl of gnashing and twisting and an alligator lunged at me. It was a lone alligator, and, being a lone alligator, looked upon that particular stretch of water as his own private domain and trespassers encroached at their peril. I lashed out with a paddle and it went back the way it came.

I was lucky. It was my first encounter with an alligator and I hoped my last. Next time I might not be so lucky. It was my own fault. I dropped my guard. I should have known that, with all my experience of paddling up and down rivers, that water is not always as it seems, that sometimes a calm surface hides turbulence underneath and lurking demons all too ready to pull you under.

Nothing much happened after that. I whistled and sang as I went along, even reciting bits of poetry from my schooldays. The Walrus and the Carpenter from Alice in Wonderland came to mind, and the verse the White Rabbit recited to the King. I smiled as I thought of Elizabeth.

*****

I was passing through some of the flattest country I had seen when below the horizon I saw a plume of smoke. It reminded me of the Wild West: Red Indians, as they used to call them, sending smoke signals in as wild and woolly a landscape as is possible to conceive outside of Texas. Forest fire probably that would burn itself out. I thought no more of it. I pressed on. My journey never seemed to end. Sunrise followed sunset, night followed day. Sweat poured off me. I kept on paddling.

Once again I lapsed into melancholy at the thought that I was alone on the island and would never see anyone again, and it was in this state of mind that I tried to convince myself that Danny, Heidi and Cora were figments of my imagination and the only reality was my dreams. Then I snapped out of it and found myself back in the rainforest.

Hornbills shrieked from the canopy above. Trees trailed their usual leafy fingers in the currents as I slipped silently along a corridor through the thick foliage. Fallen trees cluttered the banks. A wall of giant hardwoods made me catch my breath. Then I came to a break in the trees.

Dappled sunlight made patterns on a grass bank, emerald green and smooth as silk, which, with the close embrace of the forest, birdsong and the fragrance of a million exotic blooms, made a mockery of a world where life and death go hand in hand.

CHAPTER TWENTY

HOME AT LAST

I took the canoe all the way to the cabin now I knew where I was going, and tied it to a tree where the river widened and where I washed and had the occasional swim.

My intention was to build a boathouse, not as elaborate as the one in Newtown, but sufficient to dry dock the canoe and repair its damaged side as well as sheltering it from the elements. Also it would keep the monkeys away. They meant more mischief than harm but could be a nuisance sometimes.

The cabin was as I had left it. I opened the windows to let in the air, including the two doors, one I never used. It wouldn't open at first time so I put my shoulder to it and it flew back on rusty hinges.

*****

I spent the first couple of weeks sweeping and tidying up in general, and airing the beds in the off chance of getting visitors, knowing there was as much chance of that happening as Mars being in conjunction with a flying pig.

I didn't see the baboons until the third day. They came in twos and threes, suspicious at first and then came up close, some going up on their hind legs and sniffing the air as if trying to get my scent, but, of course, only dogs and the like use smell to make contact. Simians rely on sight. I greeted them with gestures to feel free to roam about as much as they liked, as this was their home as much as well as mine, except the cabin which was my private domain and out of bounds to all unless invited.

I arranged part of the cabin so as to be as comfortable as possible, the rest I ignored. The emeralds I stood on the locker by my bed next to the Bible. The stove was lit only at night. All in all, home sweet home, a place to call my own.

*****

The first night I dreamt of Heidi again - so vivid it might have been yesterday - repeating the good/evil theme, reminding me what a besotted fool I had been, exploited and manipulated beyond belief in case I forgot.

'We were going for a swim. She walked to the water's edge, hair blowing over in the wind, smiling all over her face. She was still smiling when she plunged in and disappeared beneath the waves. Frantic with worry, I dived in after her. She was a better swimmer than I gave her credit for. She took hold of my legs and pulled me under. I struggled to break the surface only to be pulled back down again. I was fighting for breath. When I finally did manage to reach the surface she stopped playing games and we both headed for the beach, me in front, her behind. I was wrapping the towel around me when a rock narrowly missed my head and buried itself in the sand. "It came from the sea," she said. "It happens sometimes."'

I didn't need reminding. That was Heidi all right, callous, scheming and mean. Maybe I asked for all I got but it wouldn't happen again, not because Heidi was dead but because I had learnt my lesson and would be extra careful the next time. Maybe it was a good thing Cora left as she did. Maybe. We'd see. I barely thought of Heidi again. As far as I was concerned she never existed.

I spent the days putting the finishing touches to the clearing and thought it would be nice to have a border of flowers around the edges, or go overboard and have flower beds and perhaps a couple of rockeries scattered around, and maybe a lawn and variegated climbing plants to hide the fence. Newtown had a lawn, swimming pool and other trappings of wealth, why shouldn't I? I was just as rich, perhaps richer, given that I was the owner of an emerald mine. Not many college lecturers can say that. Only I knew where the emeralds were and no one else.

*****

Maybe I would take another trip to Newtown, but not just yet. I wanted to get used to my own place first. In all the time I had been on the island, I had only spent a couple of months there, keeping it ship-shape to keep the encroaching jungle at bay. I didn't even give myself time to laze around. I was always fixing, mending, chopping, digging, cleaning, putting up fences, gathering fruit, rearranging furniture in the cabin to give it that 'home sweet home' feeling, and a thousand and one other chores necessary before I could really call it home. Maybe I would get round to making the hammock I promised myself. I got the idea at Elizabeth's place. I would make one in her memory.

*****

Most days the sun was too hot for me to do anything anyway, especially in the afternoons, a factor I ignored on my travels when the briefest lapse of concentration could mean the difference between life and death. Here at home, where I had more control of my movements, I could relax.

Cora entered my thoughts, as did the Bible, although the two were not connected except one preached virtue and the other put it into practice. Save for that night in the bushes - or because of it - I could not fault Cora in spite of my reservations, gleaned from experience, concerning the sincerity of women. What surprised me was she should see me in a romantic light, given that I didn't consider myself to be a lady's man, but, all things considered, that was all she could give and I did save her life, which is not saying I wasn't flattered.

*****

Although I was without a care in the world, a voice kept telling me to read the Bible if my luck were to continue. All kind of things might happen. I might be stricken with fever again, attacked by another alligator, encounter a bull that might not be so understanding, or fall off a cliff as I did in the enclave, either of which may have dire consequences. I wasn't afraid to die but didn't see any sense in tempting fate just for the sake of reading a couple of passages each day, which I did and was surprised at the conclusions I drew from them; one being I could not be happier – save for wanting to see Cora again - given that I had survived against all odds when I could have easily succumbed in such a hostile environment. I had thought of this many times but the Bible, with its clarity and thoroughness, made sure I didn't forget.

*****

It followed that if the bank robbers had intended settling on the island, they had made plans for a regular supply of food, which meant growing their own, evidence of which was the half-scratched soil, meaning they had acquired seeds; seeds that would help me grow a regular supply.

It wasn't far to the shack, two hours on foot, four hours round trip, a distance I wouldn't have dreamt of undertaking before I came to Pagp Mara, but just routine now.

I could either walk or take the canoe. If I took the canoe it depended on the weather how long it took me to get there. If I walked the baboons would accompany me some of the way; all the way if they thought I was in danger. They would know when I was ready. They knew everything else.

*****

A storm blew up. It lasted forty minutes, enough to make the river overflow its banks. Ten minutes after it blew over the river got back to normal, the animals came out of hiding, the trees were fresh and green and there was a soft breeze in the air.

As a change from wildfowl I had roebuck for lunch, way past its prime and on its last legs. A leopard would have brought it to its knees and subjected it to a slow, painful death, whereas I dispatched it quickly and mercifully.

On one of my walks through the forest I came across the remains of the two bank robbers I had condemned to the wrath of the baboons. They had barely got past the first tree before they were torn limb from limb. They were not a pretty sight.

The baboons watched as I fetched a spade from the cabin and buried what I could. What was left I kicked into the undergrowth. Where there was no evidence there was no crime. The baboons came down from the trees and danced around me on all fours, coughing and squealing with delight.

Those who say apes can't express humour the same way we do have never seen baboons at their ecstatic best. They thought that by all eradicating all traces of what they had done I approved of their behaviour, which had a touch of irony since it me who gave them the chance to kill in the first place.

CHAPTER TWENTY ONE

I DO ODD JOBS

I got into the same routine as before, only instead of hacking away at encroaching undergrowth, I passed the time doing the other chores I mentioned. As I said, tools were no object, I had one for every occasion including, glue, hacksaw, tacks, screws, garden tools and innumerable other accessories including a chain saw, the devil's own invention, which I didn't use simply because I didn't know how to; all in all a DIY enthusiast's dream.

My first job was repairing the canoe. After examining it I saw it wasn't as bad as I thought, just splintered a little when presumably it broke loose and crashed into something. It had taken me hundreds of miles and hadn't sunk yet. The adage 'If it isn't broke, don't mend it' might well have been coined that very moment. If I started messing around it might never float again, so I left well alone.

After a couple of weeks I got restless. I forced myself to relax and expunge all thoughts of travel from my mind. I had to settle down sometime. I had a home now, what more did I want? A home made from an abandoned cabin, something to call my own, warm and comfortable, and by the time I finished would rival any home if you forget radio and television, but then who wants radio and television when you have everything else at your finger-tips? As far as I was concerned the only thing missing was Cora, and it wasn't outside the realm of possibility that I would get her in the end. All I had to do was wait. I wasn't planning on going anywhere.

*****

It wasn't a bad life once I'd sorted myself out. Fits of melancholy were almost a thing of the past. I got them occasionally but no more dreams.

I found paint, brushes and paint thinner among other things buried away in lockers and cupboard. Not a day went by without I came across something that might come in useful. I arranged the paint in its respective colours outside the cabin in the shade of a tree, most of it white, the favoured colour in the tropics because it reflects the sun.

The cabin had once been white but had faded over the years. Now it was greyish-green, a colour I was in favour of as it blended with the surroundings. Not that I minded being seen. It's just that I didn't want to advertise my whereabouts to all and sundry. I only wanted one person to know in case if she wanted me she would know where to come.

I put the paint to good use by arranging cobble-stones I fetched from the beach around the cabin in the way soldiers do around their billets and painted them white. The effect was pleasantly surprising. The camp, as I called it, wasn't drab any more. It looked disciplined and orderly. I had my work cut out chasing the baboons away so they wouldn't be covered in paint and finished up covered in the stuff myself.

*****

It was beginning to look more as I wanted it to be each time I did something. I quite enjoyed myself once I got into the swing. Not only that, I didn't have time to reflect on what might have been. I didn't have time to get sad. All I had time for was getting the place looking as if it was owned by somebody who knew what he was doing, a man with a purpose in life who didn't sit back and mope.

Next I stood the canoe on its end and painted it a nice pastel blue, filling in the cracks where it had splintered with plastic glue. Not bad for a man who had never so much as picked up a screwdriver in his life. Once again the baboons were curious spectators but better behaved this time. I recalled the watch I had found and couldn't remember where I put it. It wasn't important but I couldn't deny it had a certain resonance.

A lawn in the middle of the camp would set it off nicely but where to find suitable grass? The only grass I could see was either too coarse or tall enough to hide an elephant. Now if I could find a dozen small tufts and propagate them with gentle love and care, applying liberal doses of water and shelter them from extremities of weather, I might get my lawn. They couldn't hang me for trying.

I strengthened the fence by threading shafts of bamboo through the main body. It was tedious work, long and tiring, but had to be done. It took me over a month. Sweat poured off me. I quenched my thirst with water I kept in a water butt in the shade outside the cabin. It was warm and tasted disgusting. Not so when I was on my travels, when, out of necessity, I drank from rivers and water holes, but my mind was on more pressing matters such as staying alive rather than on the delicacies of food and drink. I would have to devise a way of keeping my drinking water cool. If there was a way, I would find it.

*****

I didn't always bathe in the river. Sometimes, after a tiring day, I had a strip wash in the cabin. The weeks strengthened the fence was one such occasion. I ached all over and my back was killing me from constant bending.

Each night I washed, shaved, changed and made a fire and each night I said a little prayer. It was in these moments that I knew I wasn't alone. Someone was with me. I heard no one, saw no one yet someone was there.

As a change from fish and wildfowl I had roebuck steak and sweet corn for dinner, which I boiled in water after I fried the steak in its own fat. Fat didn't bother me, I ate as much as I liked and didn't put on an ounce of weight. The secret was I drank plenty of water, even when travelling, sometimes as much as three litres a day, sometimes more.

Water is the most important catalyst in losing weight and keeping it off, the only true magic potion for permanent weight loss. It suppresses the appetite and helps metabolise stored fat. Studies have shown that the less water we drink the more fat deposits increase, while an increase in water actually reduces fat deposits.

*****

One night in particular caused me anxiety. I had just got into bed and turned off the lamp when I was seized by panic; the darkness closed in on me pinning me down and I struggled to get free. Then I froze, I couldn't move, and in that brief moment of terror my life passed before me, and then, as if by some bewildering alchemy, I was my old self again. I sat up as if awakening from a bad dream when in fact I hadn't dreamt at all.

I sat up, threw my legs over the side of the bed and sat thinking, then got to my feet and palmed back the curtain.

A thousand luminous eyes stared back at me from out of the gloom and suddenly I saw the funny side and burst out laughing. Before I got back in bed I had hot cocoanut milk with honey I risked being stung to death to obtain as I dived into a river to escape the bees, the honey wrapped in a plastic bag.

The glowing stove cast patterns over the beds like shrouds over pagan altars. I heard someone calling but no one was there. A little soft music to lull me back to sleep wouldn't be amiss, but you can't have everything. I was on my Island of Dreams, what more did I want?

*****

I slept soundly and awoke the next morning to the usual dawn chorus of twittering birds and chattering monkeys. After breakfast I went outside and examined my handiwork. The canoe looked new; I had done a decent job all around. The cobblestones were reminiscent of an army camp, which was my intention. The fence needed prettying up, however. As I said, climbing plants should do the trick. It shouldn't be too difficult coaxing them out of the undergrowth.

As luck would have it parts of the fence were near the jungle edge. I attached trailing stems of a climbing plant not unlike the clematis to the bamboo uprights and let nature do the rest. I didn't expect results overnight. It would take time for them to take hold. Eventually I hoped to have pink and blue flowers encircling the camp like a garland.

*****

Nothing happened for the next three months then

the clematis started to make its mark. The baboons, who had been absent for some time, started coming back in twos and threes. I didn't mind. They were free to roam as much as they liked. With them came all manner of jungle life suspicious of the clematis that had moved from its usual place, ready to flee at the slightest sign of danger.

CHAPTER TWENTY TWO

I DIG MY FIRST GARDEN

It was late morning. The noise was deafening. I ran out of the cabin and looked up. The rotor blades of a helicopter blew up swirls of loose soil as it came down and hovered between the trees. It stayed like that for several minutes before rising above the canopy and fading out of view.

I didn't take a lot of notice but I was curious all the same. Was it the same helicopter I had seen before? Was I being spied upon? I could understand the transformation of an abandoned wilderness into what would seem like a holiday camp from the air arousing the curiosity to such an extent as to risk taking a closer look, but not why they didn't go the whole hog and come down where I could answer any questions they cared to ask.

The possibility occurred to me that perhaps I was on the island illegally; that it was a protectorate under the jurisprudence of the Australian government or some other government, who were legally bound to administer to its well being and maintain law and order as far as was appropriate. If no one knew I was there apart from Cora, they did now.

Perhaps I should have made my home in a cave where no one would see me instead of taking up residence near a the sea that would lure tourists like bees to a honey pot. If Newtown was anything to go by, tourists were already taking over and looking at me from a helicopter was their way of getting acquainted. I looked forward to meeting them. If the helicopter was from a government department, I would either be ordered to leave the island or ignored as if I wasn't there.

*****

I made preparations for my journey to the bank robbers' shack hoping to pick up vegetable seeds and anything else I might find. The baboons gathered in force as I slung the machete across my back and checked my knife and axe. I wouldn't need the compass even if it worked as I wouldn't be gone for more than a two days. It wasn't more than an eight-hour round trip on foot; a day and night at the most if I decided to bed down for the night. I took a bin-liner I found in a cupboard to carry what I might find and set off.

Typically, the baboons accompanied me part of the way they turned back where there were no trees. Although they were not tree monkeys in the strictest sense, they were, however, arboreal by instinct and felt vulnerable when there was nothing to climb.

*****

The shack was the same as I left it, dirty, smelly, insects still scurrying around, fat spiders still picking over dead flies and damp enough to cultivate mushrooms. I rummaged around. My journey wasn't wasted. I found packets of seed, dozens of them, and various bulbs and roots. The packets illustrated what kind of the seeds they were. The roots didn't need explaining. The bulbs kept their identity to themselves. I put them all in the bag.

The bank robbers had done well considering they probably knew less about gardening than I did. It was unfortunate the same wisdom failed them when they decided to take me on. It was their biggest and final mistake. In a way I felt sorry for them but they asked for what they got, including Danny, who was probably the worst of all. I put the seeds etc. in the bin-liner.

Even though the shack hadn't been empty long, the rainforest was already reclaiming the ground it stood on, thanks to the fruit bat whose contribution to the eco-system is to propagate growth by depositing pollen on damaged parts of the forest so that plant-life may grow again.

*****

I was on my way back through the trees when I sensed I was being followed. I eased the machete out of the sheath as the faint rustle of leaves carried on the silent air followed by the almost imperceptible creaking of a branch.

Out of the corner of my eye I saw a leopard above me ready to spring. In the instant it braced itself I dodged behind a tree and shot back into view screaming at the top of my voice at the same time chopping the air with the machete like a madman. It worked. The leopard, startled that I had taken the initiative instead of waiting for him to make the first move, was at a loss what to do, so like the other turned tail and ran.

If I had panicked, given that he had the advantage, he would have taken me. Conversely, one to one on the ground without the machete, I would have taken him. The thing is I kept my cool. If only people knew that the ridiculous resolutions made in the grip of fear deprives them of the use of those means which reason offers for their relief, panic would be a thing of the past.

*****

I spent the following week weeding and digging vegetable beds. I knew that raising plants from seed is a risky business, and if you're a beginner like me you're better off buying plants that have been raised in a nursery. But since there was no nursery for more than a thousand miles, I had no choice but to rely on common sense and the optimism that had got me this far.

I marked out different sections for different vegetables and raked the soil surface to a fine tilth before sowing seed broadcast in the simplest outdoor method and then planted potatoes and other root vegetables and built a frame for the tomatoes, dampening it all down. I then strung bits of paper cut from the magazines over the seeds to keep the birds away.

Bearing in mind the ferocity of the storms and the damage they wreak, I looked around for something that would hold the soil together; strips of wood etc. I could dig in and compact each section.

I found a pile of seasoned wood in the trees behind the cabin that had been dumped and forgotten. Sawing them into strips was long and tiring, but once the job was done I was more than pleased with the results. Congratulations apart, I had a lot more to do to make my little fortification the way I wanted it. I was lucky to have the baboons as friends; they were the best 'guard dogs' in the world. In spite of they lived deep in the jungle, they were never far away.

I had an urge to visit the beach again, not to mull over old times but to feel the sea breeze in my face, hear the cry of the gulls and scan the vast ocean and horizon beyond.

I locked the cabin and was on my way. A baboon

accompanied me so far and left me when he felt I was safe. Even then I could feel his eyes on me.

CHAPTER TWENTY THREE

FRIEND OR FOE?

The realisation that I had been very lucky came back to me as a warning that a lapse of wariness might be my undoing. The fact that I had travelled the island with impunity didn't mean that it would last forever. Anything might happen. There is something to be said for not taking things for granted; that good fortune is a birthright and something to glory in as if it were an achievement to be born. One must keep a sense of proportion and bear in mind that nothing, even luck, lasts forever.

It was with these thoughts in mind that I emerged from the jungle and walked along the beach keeping well away from the water's edge. What happened to the seal at the foot of the cliffs came back to me.

Sharks feeding inshore and killer whales hugging the coastline do it for one reason and one reason only – to leap out and snatch what they can. Many an unwary beachcomber has finished up in the jaws of death without knowing what was happening.

I glanced at where Heidi was buried over by the trees and it was with no small measure of self-reproach that I considered going over to take a look. 'Self-reproach' because I resolved never to think of her again and there I was contemplating paying homage as if she still meant something to me. The only explanation I can give is some memories, even bad memories, are hard to erase, and when finally they are it seems as if they never happened. Even now memories were getting fainter. Soon they would be no more, and Heidi would firmly and indubitably be part of the past.

*****

As I walked I could see where the beach gave way to rocks where the cliffs took over. Lapping water came from a jumble of rocks ahead of me. At the water's edge a tussle was taking place that got more frenetic as I got nearer. Squawks mingled with growls.

A civet cat, not unlike the domestic cat, with an unusually small head, sharp features and short legs, had hold of an albatross; a goose look-alike with white plumage tinged with yellow, and was dragging it away from the sea where it was struggling to reach. A solitary bird, it is renowned for flying long distances and, being a strong swimmer, has webbed feet, and a sharply hooked beak. But the civet had rendered it useless by hanging on to its tail. It was either injured or exhausted after a long flight and had come down to rest when the civet, usually found in wooded areas, was scavenging for food among the rocks and happened on it unexpectedly.

When it saw me the civet loosened its grip and the albatross plunged into the sea in desperation. The civet plunged in after it. A couple of well-aimed rocks sent it on its way. The albatross still wasn't safe. Too weak to swim, it was caught in the incoming tide. I fished it out and laid it gently on the beach and watched over it until it had completely recovered in case the civet came back. In no time it was on its feet preening itself and then, after a short run, took to the air effortlessly and gracefully.

According to the law of the jungle, I should have left it to its fate but I was human and couldn't just walk away leaving it to be ripped to pieces. I was also a hypocrite. If I had been as hungry as the civet I would have eaten it myself.

*****

I was on my way back to my cabin when presumably the same helicopter that had visited me before came from nowhere, hovered over me as it did the last time and disappeared in exactly the same way.

To say I was puzzled is an understatement. I wouldn't have been so concerned if I had known where it was from or why it was acting the way it did. It is the not knowing that is worrying. Maybe its next stop was my cabin. If I was being spied upon, the ones doing the spying would know it would take me at least two hours to get back to my cabin, in which time they could take over the place and claim it as their own, if the baboons let them. They wouldn't just stand by and do nothing.

My imagination ran wild, conjuring up any number of ifs and buts until finally common sense prevailed. Petty thieves don't ride around in helicopters looking for isolated cabins in the jungle and anything else they can lay their hands on. The only explanation I could think of was they wanted to find out who I was and what I was doing there.

I took my time. I would feel foolish if I hurried back and no one was waiting for me. Then I thought that if the baboons were around they wouldn't dare land, or if they did wouldn't dare get out of the helicopter unless, of course, they had firearms. That was the excuse I needed. I followed the same path back as I came in double quick time.

*****

My little fortification was as I had left it except for a circle of flattened grass similar to the one at Newtown. I'd had visitors, after all. But they didn't inspect the cabin. They didn't inspect anything. They stayed in the helicopter probably because the baboons were hanging around but not any more. They had done their good deed for the day and made themselves scarce, but I knew they were there if needed.

As if reading my thoughts they emerged from the trees and gathered around, jumping up and down excitedly. They were trying to tell me something, and it was only when I looked beyond them that I saw two food hampers and a familiar circle of flattened grass I didn't need a crystal ball to tell me had been made by a helicopter; and its passengers, seeing the baboons, didn't land for fear of being attacked and had dumped them there.

I examined them. They hadn't been tampered with, which was surprising since curiosity is part of the baboon's nature until I remembered I was their friend, you could say their leader, and they regarded my place as hallowed ground where even being there was considered a great honour, never mind touch anything.

When they saw I intended picking one up, they did their best to help but were more of a hindrance than anything. Still, the thought was there. I carried the hampers to the cabin on my shoulders as the baboons danced around excitedly. I was reminded of children at a Christmas party looking forward to their presents. Unfortunately, I had nothing to give them.

They kept their distance outside the cabin. A young one, sitting on its mother's back and eschewing maternal protection in favour of satisfying its curiosity, ventured over the threshold only to be hauled back by an admonishing parent.

I patted the infant's head to show there were no hard feelings and dismissed them courteously. They trundled away in their usual formation of twos and threes, chattering as they went.

I opened the first hamper. Enough food to feed ten men for a week was staring me in the face. I unpacked it, and the first items I saw were eggs and bacon packed separately. I wondered why.

I put it all in the food cupboard, including tinned soup, baked beans ham, corned beef and many more including fresh vegetables, bread, tea, coffee, powdered milk, butter, cooking fat, jam, sausages etc. and a few luxuries like cake and chocolate. There were pots and pans, boxes of matches and other essentials such as washing-up liquid, scented soap, tooth past, razor blades, you name it and, surprise surprise, a stirrup pump. Now how did they know, storms apart, the difficulty I had refilling the water butt?

Now all I had to do now was channel the water from the river like the gold prospectors of old, only instead of making conduits out of nails and wood, I split shafts of bamboo thicker than a man's arm lengthways and mounted them on stilts dug into the ground in perfect alignment, like steps going downwards, to facilitate a constant flow. Instead of getting calluses filling it by hand with a pail, I got corns pumping water with my foot.

Of course, prettying things up with clematis would be self-defeating if an ugly conduit were to run through the camp unless I devised a means of dismantling it when not in use, but I didn't need to. The water butt stood on the edge of the clearing nearest the river so the conduit was hidden in the trees.

*****

It was all very well making plans for the future when my first priority should have been asking who the people in the helicopter were, and what reason did they have for providing for my welfare, not to mention the gesture of the stirrup pump, the need of which no one should know about apart from myself? It was all very puzzling as if someone was privy to what I did and what I was going to do.

I compared my present position with what would have happened had Irvie had not visited me. Taken a professorship at a top college, I guess, and grow old watching my whiskers grow. I would certainly have got rid of Heidi. As it was, I had not only made a new life for myself but had established a home and friends. Even my enemies respected me. If I didn't let it go to my head I might live to a ripe old age.

CHAPTER TWENTY FOUR

A FRIEND FOR LIFE

Green shoots poked their heads above the soil in the vegetable patch and the clematis was spreading its stalks in every direction like tentacles. The hot sun promoted growth and I watered them regularly. In the dry season, when storms were few and far between, watering took up a lot of my time even with the stirrup pump. I watered the plants that were out of reach by throwing water from a pail at an angle high in the air so the water came down in a fine spray and didn't disturb the surface soil.

The tomato plants were halfway up the frame and the first of the potatoes were beginning to show. It is not for reasons of modesty that I attribute this remarkable success to climate rather than gardening skill because I had no gardening skill. All I did was follow the logic of reason and common sense and let nature do the rest. I even painted the water butt green. My little fortification looked more like the Garden of Eden with each passing day.

*****

Two months went by before the helicopter paid me another visit. Coincidence or not, I wasn't at home again, and knew it had called because of the familiar 'crop circle' and two more hampers in the same spot the other two deliveries had been made. The contents were more or less the same save for there was no stirrup pump. The baboons were as excited as before and so followed a re-enactment of what had taken place previously, except the mother kept a tight hold on her baby.

As the weeks went by their numbers dwindled to a few stragglers but I knew in an emergency they would be at my side like a shot. It had happened before when other monkeys took their place.

I got the usual visitors like the old boar who came once a week to root around, a family of squirrels that came every day and noted everything that went on from the safety of a tree, and a guinea fowl and her chicks that passed through when it suited her as if she owned the place. It was amusing the way every one of them they avoided the vegetable patch I had effectively got through to them as a no-go area.

*****

It was my habit to make a fire in the evening to keep the cabin warm during the night, so it was no trouble putting fresh logs on the fire in the morning and having egg and bacon for breakfast. I had more food than I knew what to do with. I had never eaten so well.

But I mustn't get smug. There's always a price to pay. Having got used to the good life, I hoped I could readjust when the helicopter stopped coming as easily as when I first came to the island. But things were different then. I was a man possessed, fighting to survive, with a cast-iron will and something to prove. Now things were different and I had nothing to prove, but I mustn't let complacency stand in my way. The moment I did I was finished.

*****

I visited the mire where Heidi made lying excuses about her relationship with Danny. I didn't altogether believe her and by the time I was proved right it was too late. I was a fool then; maybe I was a fool now. My feeling for Cora on so short an acquaintance was proof of this but I could be wrong.

The two rocks I had smashed were still there, as was the doomed roebuck caught in the thicket. Nothing had changed; it was still bleak and brooding and the longer I sat there the more miserable I became. The time to snap out of and take stock of myself was now. No one else could do it for me. I was my own person accountable to no one but myself, and if I made mistakes it was on my own head and no one but me could say they had a hand in it.

*****

Whimpers came from behind me. I searched the undergrowth and came upon a wild dog, a bitch, lying on her side with her throat torn out. Three puppies lay beside her who had suffered the same fate. Two other puppies had survived. They were huddled under a thick tangle of roots out of harm's way. It took time and patience to coax them out and the blink of an eye pushing them back in as sixth sense told me all was not well.

I stood up, turned and drew the machete all in one movement, and what I saw prepared me for the fight of my life. Not known to show mercy, no other animal expresses more clearly in terms of pictorial action the delights of violence and a connoisseur of the quick kill: The wolverine, or, as it is called in Europe, the glutton.

A rodent, just over a metre long, with bear-like characteristics, it walks with a menacing, sinewy gait and at times seems to be walking sideways. It kills without compunction and knows no fear. Reports that a single wolverine can scatter a pack of Canadian timber wolves and steals their food from under their noses seems to support this view. This one was either too old or too tired. It certainly wasn't hungry. It ignored me.

*****

I took the puppies home and thought bread and milk were the right things to give them until they spat it out and then I realised they were robust enough to eat meat and other fare. I put them at roughly two months old, which is equivalent to a year-old domestic dog that doesn't have to forage and kill for food. If the wild dog took this long to mature the species would have died out long ago.

They flourished under my tender, loving care to the chagrin of the baboons who saw them as a threat to their role as number one, and would have killed them given half the chance. But once I got through to them that the puppies had their own part to play in camp life they treated them with as much tolerance as their nature would allow.

One of the puppies died. He was the weaker one and passed away peacefully in his sleep. The surviving one, I called her Shandy, had one paw over her brother's face as if protecting him from life itself. She wouldn't move from his side until I assured her that I meant no harm, and buried him quickly as I could in the trees under the customary rocks and stones to deter predators.

As time went by, Shandy adapted to a life of obedience and domesticity with remarkable fortitude, remarkable since she came from a stock unfettered and untamed since time began.

House-training wasn't as difficult as I thought. Each time she made a mess I rubbed her nose in it and gently but firmly plonked her on a bed of dry grass I placed just inside the door. When she got used to it I moved the grass outside the door. She fell down the steps a couple of times but soon got the hang of it, and in no time found her own private spot among the trees.

She soon grew sturdy and strong and got on well with the baboons, after a fashion. It took time for them to get used to the idea that I gave her what they considered preferential treatment by allowing her to sleep inside the cabin, especially since they had always regarded it as taboo to venture even as far as the steps. She was faster than they were in a straight run but they had the edge in most other things.

They could climb and swing through the trees, were stronger and deadly fighters. Shandy had more energy and in many ways was more intelligent but, paradoxically, couldn't figure things out for herself. She wouldn't go near the vegetable patch, for instance, because I told her not to. The baboons, on the other hand, didn't because they reasoned stamping feet ruined crops, and the other animals followed suit.

*****

Five weeks passed before my benefactors called again. I don't need to say I wasn't at home. This time they added ten bags of fertiliser to the two hampers. I hadn't worked my way through the second hamper of the first consignment yet, let alone two more to add to the two I already had. Although there was variety, I augmented it with fresh meat and fish caught in the usual way perhaps to prove, if only to myself, that I wasn't exactly dependent on hand-outs. The 'perishables', the stuff that had gone bad, I threw in the river, and dug a deep hole for the empty tincans, which I flattened and covered them with layers of top soil to deter scavengers.

I scattered the fertiliser over the vegetable patch which would increase the chances of growing my own vegetables, thanks to the visiting angels – there must be more than one – whom I hoped to meet one day if only to say thank you. When the baboons weren't around, that is.

Although the baboons were my friends, they didn't look very friendly and could be dangerous when provoked, which was why I always took Shandy with me unless it was a short trip and then I locked her in the cabin. Perhaps when they got to know each other, I would give her more freedom.

*****

One day found me doing what I had meant to do since moving into the cabin, and that was clean it from top to bottom. I started with the beds, lockers and tables, moving them to one side while I swept and mopped the floor, and moving them to the other side where I swept and mopped again.

As well as dust and cobwebs, there were magazines, socks, combs and sundry other things. Shandy enjoyed herself, moving from place to place in order to keep out of my way and growling at the least little thing. I vowed I would never put her on a lead. She was a free agent as far as discretion would allow. I wouldn't tell her what to do and where to go. She had a mind of her own. She was an intelligent dog.

Next I cleaned the windows and put up clean

curtains, putting the old ones with the rest of the dirty laundry I washed each week and hung out to dry under the burning sun.

I fell into a routine that I rigorous adhered to even if I didn't always feel up to it. I was a hard task master almost to the point of masochism, on the premise that if I didn't maintain a certain standard of cleanliness I might as well join the monkeys in the trees. I washed the walls and gave the lockers a fresh lick of paint; all twenty of them, black leaded the stove and painted a white square round it military style. In point of fact I modelled the entire camp on the lines of an army base. Discipline is the thing. It was the only way to survive.

It took me the best part of three weeks to get the camp as I wanted it, though a lot still needed doing. Three weeks sounds a long time, yet nothing compared to a lifetime keeping it that way. I painted the cobblestones again, more as a lesson in obedience for Shandy's benefit rather than they needed it. As I said, discipline is the thing and in order to instil absolute obedience I chastised her once or twice for sniffing the paint when I told her not to.

The baboons were puzzled by my behaviour. They were lucky; their parents had brought them up. I was bringing up Shandy in the only way I knew how and teaching her what I considered necessary if she were to take care of herself when I was no longer round was the mainstay of the curriculum.

*****

One afternoon I skirted the perimeter of the camp with Shandy at my heels and a couple of baboons trailing behind, thinking not for the first time how lucky I was;

from college lecturer to hunter-gatherer who owned an emerald mine on a remote South Pacific island surrounded by friends in an environment partly of my own making and in which I was comfortable. I could leave the island and conquer the world any time I chose. I could have people dance attendance, pandering to me every whim. I could have everything I ever wanted. But all I wanted was to be left in peace with my friends, and Cora if she was around.

*****

I heard a helicopter in the distance. It got nearer and I could tell by the tremendous noise that it was flying low. Then it appeared and thousands of birds took to the air in a cacophony of flapping wings. It began its descent, the huge rotor blades shearing the leaves like confetti as it narrowly missed the trees like some monstrous insect homing down on its prey. Then, rising up again, it got its bearings and came down between the cabin and the vegetable patch, a cumbersome, swaying hunk of metal that landed as gently and unhurriedly as a butterfly.

The baboons shot off into the trees. Shandy was shaking with fear. I picked her up and went to meet my benefactors.

CHAPTER TWENTY FIVE

ANSWERS TO MY QUESTIONS

I put Shandy down as the door swung open and a tall, fair-haired man got out, followed by a well-dressed, middle-aged couple he helped down the steps. They were his parents, judging not only on looks but the way he fussed around. They glanced around and what started as an expression of pleasant surprise collapsed into something akin to disappointment.

They weren't the only ones that were surprised. The baboons and other animals, emerging from the foliage, were surprised too, and stood gaping at the visitors as if they were aliens from outer space. They might well have been aliens from outer space for I was the only human most of the animals had seen. The baboons, suspicious of everything and everybody, were fidgety and mumbling to each other.

I spoke first. "Nothing's going to happen to you, don't worry. They mean you no harm," adding conversationally, "I take it it was you who dropped the supplies. What I can't figure is how did you know I needed a stirrup pump?" I was conscious of my torn shirt. "If I'd known you were coming I'd have smartened myself up. It's not every day I get visitors," then turned to the woman who was focused on the vegetable patch. "Take a closer look. Maybe you can tell me where I went wrong. I'm not cut out to be a gardener."

She was only too glad to do something and went

over, father and son following like sheep.

She examined the various sections with a critical eye. "For someone who is not a gardener," she said, "you've done an excellent job except there are no markers showing what's what. The tomatoes are the only ones I can identify."

It was a lame excuse but better than none. "I forgot. The seeds were in packets with illustrations of what they were, so I've no excuse. Not that it matters. I'll take anything that grows."

The baboons thinned out and dispersed. Others followed.

The woman pointed at the Chontas trees. "What are those?"

"Chontas trees," I replied, "created by the devil for the devil and feared by sinners and non-sinners alike, the most fiendish tree in existence. Barbed wire in full bloom, I call them."

She pulled a face. "Ugh!"

"That's what I thought."

The old man admonished her. "Julie, what on earth are you doing?"

She pulled another face. "You're lucky I didn't spit."

What baboons there were calmed down except for a mother and her baby who was crying. I went over, and, smiling gently, took the baby from her and cradled it gently in my arms until it stopped crying before giving it back. I did it casually and with such compassion as if I did it every day. Actually it was my first time and was as surprised as anyone at the results. Baboons are jealous mothers who will kill rather than let anyone get within arm's length of their babies yet there I was not only getting away with it, but with the blessing of the mother.

The woman didn't take her eyes off me. She wanted

to do the same but, of course, it was out of the question. It wasn't that she was in any way less than a mother herself, but in the baboon's eyes a stranger who might mean the baby harm. I was different. I was their leader.

She cheered up a little. The rictus of a familiar smile I couldn't identify fleetingly passed over face, her eyes lit up. "What an amazing man you are."

I didn't say anything. I invited them to the cabin. Shandy followed. Once or twice the woman tried to stroke her but she was having none of it. Like the baboons, she was suspicious of strangers and had to get to know them first.

The two men trailed behind. It was mid-afternoon and at its hottest. The woman passed the old man a handkerchief and he wiped his neck and face. The younger man produced his own handkerchief and wiped his own neck and face. The woman was cool and didn't need handkerchief.

*****

They were impressed by my arrangement of beds and lockers neatly aligned, windows set off by pretty curtains, floor covered with carpets, enough food for an army, sink unit, toilet accessories, an old tea urn I found and kept filled with drinking water, and tables and chairs set around the stove all nice and cosy.

The young man made the introductions. "My father and mother. I'm Peter Benson."

I smiled. "Pleased to meet you. My name's Kieron."

We shook hands. It didn't dawn on me to ask what they were doing there. Before we got settled I asked if they would like tea. When they said yes, they were embarrassed that I had to light the stove to boil the kettle, so I salved any feelings of guilt they may have had about putting me to a lot of trouble by explaining fire was the only means I had of boiling water, and it had become second nature and no longer a chore, assuring them it was no trouble at all.

Now her fears were behind her, the woman was as I imagined her to be; energetic, younger than her years, which I put in her early sixties. She jumped up and, with an enthusiasm that surprised no one but me, volunteered to light the stove.

"I haven't lit a fire since I was in my early twenties," she enthused, looking at her husband with a loving smile. "We had only been married six months. That was before a rich uncle died and left me his entire fortune, which included a chain of hotels and vineyards in France."

Another loving smile. "Our dream came true, Henry, and I'm as happy as when we first met. I've never stopped being happy because I love you and will always love you."

A more unabashed declaration of love I had yet to hear.

Then she smiled. "So you see, young man, we are not short of money."

It wasn't said to belittle or embarrass me. It was the plain, simple truth without guilt or mumbling excuses.

She added proudly, "This is our son, Peter."

Peter smiled. "We've already met, mother."

She looked surprised. "Where?"

"When we got out of the helicopter," he reminded her.

She buried her face in her hands to hide her embarrassment. "Of course, how silly of me. Anyhow, about that fire, where do you keep the coal."

"You'll have to make do with logs," I replied. "The next delivery is not until next week."

Her husband saw the joke. "You've met your match, Julie."

"Keep quiet, Henry," she snapped and looked back at me. "The logs – where are they?" She rubbed her hands together. "This is going to be fun."

"Before we go any further," I said, "would you mind telling me who you are? I don't get many visitors and the few I do get I like to get acquainted."

She flushed with embarrassment again. "How rude of me. You know Cora?"

I nodded. "What about her?"

"She's our daughter. She told us everything about you and we decided to check you out for ourselves. She said you were very brave, every inch a gentleman."

I didn't entirely agree but didn't say so.

"But she does exaggerate a little," she added, "like her father."

The old man laughed.

"She said you saved her life by seeing off a leopard. Is that true."

"I'm afraid so."

"You took on a leopard!" she exclaimed.

"That's my story and I'm sticking to it."

Father and son couldn't help but smile.

She looked me up and down. "You're certainly big enough. Where do you keep the logs?" she repeated.

I pointed at the scuttle. "There."

"Thank you."

Without further preamble she cleaned out the ashes from the stove and put them in an old can I kept for that purpose. It didn't look right, a woman her age, but you could see she had done it before, a long time ago.

"What do you use for paper?" she asked.

"Dry grass and twigs. You'll find all you want under the logs."

She put a handful of dry grass in the stove, fed strips of dry twig on top followed by logs. "Matches?"

I passed her the tinder-box.

She looked at it. "What do I do with this?"

Father and son smiled again.

"You light it," I replied.

Without another word she held out her hand and the old man passed her a box of matches. She struck one, the grass took hold and in not time flames were licking upwards towards the chimney. She shut both top and bottom and clapped her hands. "There, that's done. Water?"

I filled the kettle from the tea urn and passed it to her.

"Thank you." She put it on the stove.

We sat around waiting.

*****

The afternoon wore on. We had a meal of corned beef, boiled egg, spring onion and more tea. The mug looked out of place in her hand as did everything else; the chair she sat on, table, stove, the whole set-up. It was as if they had been built around her and she was playing a part. But she was happy, and that was all that mattered.

She excused herself without saying where she was going, and I was worried about her safety until Shandy got in step beside her halfway across the clearing. She not only let the woman stroke her but seemed to revel in the attention she was getting. They were joined by a couple of baboons on the return journey. As remarkable as the baboons' affinity with a complete stranger was the woman's confident and laid back manner which was in stark contrast to the fear she exhibited twenty minutes earlier. We saw everything from a window.

Who was leading who was anybody's guess.

"They know you already, mother," the young man said when she got back.

"I feel as if I've known them all my life," came the reply. She sat down, closed her eyes and fell asleep.

Father and son laid her on a bed and then we sat outside watching the sun go down.

*****

Rain forced father and son to go to bed too. I followed suit after banking up the fire, leaving the top open so it wouldn't burn out before the morning.

They had thoughtfully left my bed for me. It was the only one made up. I put blankets over father and son and they didn't snore once. I lay awake for hours. The flickering fire made crazy patterns on the walls and ceiling. I didn't dream, hallucinate, nothing. I had one of the best night's sleep since coming to the island.

CHAPTER TWENTY SIX

I LOSE MY TEMPER

The next morning found me taking my customary dip in the river. I had left my guests sleeping, with the stove burning to ward off the morning chill. Julie, as I preferred to call her although only to myself since I didn't wish to appear presumptuous and familiar, was sleeping like a baby and looked a great deal younger than she had a right to considering she had a son around my age. I hardly knew her, indeed, I didn't know her at all, but I bet she was the life and soul of the party. Her energy belied her age, and it was easy to see she had once been pretty.

With these thoughts running through my mind, I climbed out on to the grass bank and dried myself, wrapping the towel around me in case someone was watching; a flattering thought since who would want to look at my naked body? Heidi didn't, who, in fact, was my first love and Cora my second, who more than made up for lost time by as vehement a demonstration of unbridled passion as is possible to imagine.

*****

I was so deep in thought I didn't hear Henry coming. He caught me napping, so to speak, and there I was boasting to myself how alert I was. He looked younger when sleeping too, and younger still as he sat on the grass bank beside me. My nakedness didn't bother him. I doubt if he noticed. But I put my clothes on all the same.

He was the first to speak. "I haven't seen Julie looking so happy for years; takes me back to when we were courting, in particular the morning we got the telegram saying her rich uncle had passed away." He laughed. "She had never heard of him, never mind not know him. We had a letter from a solicitor, and a month later she was a millionaire, or, as she would say 'millionairess'. She's not a feminist but doesn't like to be delineated in the male gender as if women were pale imitations. She says there would be no conflict between the sexes if each party performed the function prescribed for it by nature, and that goes for names too. She is a strong-willed woman with a mind of her own."

I nodded. "I can believe that. What are you doing here? Do you have a place on the island?" I asked.

He said, "Our second home, you might say. four hundred miles north of here in an old trading post called Newtown where the river runs into the sea. We converted the Commissionaire's house into a luxury home; swimming pool, tennis court, you name it, we've even got our own electricity and installed central locking and electric fencing to keep out intruders, not that there's any need for it. There's no on the island to keep it secure from."

"There's me," I reminded him.

He laughed. "You have everything you need here."

"I didn't always have," I argued. "I could have come across it on my travels."

He laughed again. "If you do, make yourself at home, only lay off the whisky. I forgot to get fresh supplies."

It would serve no purpose telling him I had been there except perhaps sour our friendship and give him the impression that I wasn't quite honest and couldn't be trusted. I bit into a carrot, no big deal, but he might not agree. Appearances were important if I were to see

Cora again. But first I must determine where she was.

I broke the silence. "Four hundred miles is a long way to travel by canoe," I said.

He smiled "Depends who you're travelling with,"

"I usually travel alone."

The smile lingered "And when you're not alone?"

"I take someone with me."

*****

Conversation petered out. The old boy gazed at the river lost in thought. He was a big man, had been bigger, but had shrunk with age. I put him in the same age group as Irvie. He was fitter than Irvie, though, not given to life in the city, in fact fitter than most men his age.

I wanted to know more about Cora but how without sounding nosey? Then something caught his eye, interrupting his thoughts and I saw my chance.

"How old is Cora?" I asked.

"She's our baby," he replied, "ten years younger than Peter."

"Is she in the habit of travelling alone in the rainforest?" I questioned. "I'm not looking for medals but you know what would have happened if I hadn't come along? She might have been killed."

"And we thank you from the bottom of our hearts," he said. "That's why we dumped the hampers, our way of thanking you – 'dumped' being the operative word on account of we couldn't leave the helicopter because of those damned monkeys - but that's not the end of it. We mean to give you a reward commensurate with the gratitude we feel."

I thought he was patronising and lost my temper. "I'm not looking for a reward," I snapped, "so forget it. If that's the reason you dumped them, as you call it, you can take them back. I don't need handouts. I've managed this far without them."

He was as profuse in his apology as he was dismayed that he had upset me. "Sorry if I annoyed you. I didn't mean it the way it sounded. Cora's our only daughter, and if it weren't for you we wouldn't have a daughter, surely that's easy to understand. The hampers mean nothing, merely a token gesture of the way we feel. At least allow us to show our gratitude in a more deserving way. She's fond of you," he added with a twinkle in his eye. "She talks about nothing else."

I felt better already.

"Tell me about yourself," he said. "What you're doing here, how you survive and what were you doing hundreds of miles away in a canoe when you met Cora."

"Lucky I did," I replied.

"I know," he said, "and I repeat: We owe you."

I knew I had taken things the wrong way and it was my turn to apologise. "Sorry, I'm just jumpy, I guess though I don't see why unless you took me by surprise. I'd like to see Cora again if that's all right with you," I added.

He stood up and dusted himself down. "That's what I wanted to hear. Julie said you would."

"But first," I said, "tell me what she was doing alone in the rainforest."

"Over breakfast," he replied, "I promise. I can smell egg and bacon. Coming?"

CHAPTER TWENTY SEVEN

BREAKFAST IN STYLE

Although I kept the cabin tidy, it was cleaner than usual and I didn't need to be told that Julie was responsible.

The table, decked out with a blue and white check tablecloth, was laid fit for a king. Bone china and silverware were very much in evidence. There was egg and bacon, buttered toast, marmalade, jam, coffee and a pot of tea.

It had taken time and effort to get it ready, and I didn't need to be told that Julie had done it all on her own. Little touches stood out that were the hallmark of 'a woman's touch'.

Four chairs were placed neatly on each side of the table and a transistor radio played in the background. We sat down. Things were happening that fast I was in a bit of a daze.

Henry said, "Surprised, hey? That was the idea, to keep you talking so it could be got ready. The china, silverware and bits and pieces were hidden away on the helicopter. We believe that anything worth doing is worth doing properly, and only the best will do. The toaster, percolator and radio are battery operated. We wanted to surprise you. Promise not to snap at me again," he added.

The words had barely left his mouth when he realised he should have kept it shut.

I was a little embarrassed and didn't know what to say.

Julie poured tea or coffee according to individual taste and looked meaningfully at him. "What do you mean, Henry, 'promise not to snap at me'? Has he not been a gentleman throughout?"

To avert what might develop into an argument, I spoke up. "I lost my temper; the heat probably. Forget it."

Nothing more was said. They bowed their heads in prayer before starting their meal and I followed their example. Not that I was a hypocrite. It's just that because I didn't express my beliefs openly I decried anyone who did.

*****

We ate silently. I made a pig of myself, I'm afraid. When we had finished Henry went over to the emeralds.

"What have we here?" he cried, looking in my direction. "May I?"

"You may look at them as much as you like," I told him, "after you've answered my question. What was Cora doing in the rainforest?"

He sat back down. Julie cleared the table and sat beside him. They made a handsome couple as they linked arms. Peter was only half interested as if he had heard it all before but was too polite to say so.

Without any introductory remark, Henry began. I was as interested in his telling the story as I was in the story itself, but presently, as the story unfolded, I found myself a little perturbed that a young woman should be allowed to place herself in a position where her life was in danger.

Cora was twenty three-years-old and had always been interested in rainforests and the eco-system much the same as myself, only instead of enrolling in a university to pursue the subject and possibly an academic career, she went on a year's survival course in Sarawak. Her brother went too but his heart wasn't in it; camping out in rainforests and threshing through thick undergrowth didn't appeal to him, but he still accompanied her whenever she 'hit the trail' as she put it, which meant cruising up and down the rivers in a motor-boat. She wasn't allowed to go on her own but it didn't stop her making the occasional trip when no one was looking.

She knew what she was doing, she said, and in no more danger in the rainforest than walking the streets of a big city. An assertion a little off the mark seeing that if I hadn't heard her cries the leopard would have had her.

Peter continued where his father left off. "Cora's no David Attenborough, more Charlotte Uhlenbroek without a camera crew. She would always be tramping through the rainforest if we let her. I must admit though, where you or I might get our heads bit off, she rarely sustains more than a few cuts and bruises. We have a map of every river on the island and it's possible to get here bypassing the Grand Rapids, and she can handle the motor-boat almost as well as I can so be prepared, anything might happen."

I pretended I didn't hear him. "Leopards do more than cut and bruise," I said. "Where is she now?"

"Newtown."

"Anyone with her?"

"No."

I almost exploded. "Is that wise? Anything might happen. How do you know she's not out walking in the rainforests this very moment?"

He smiled as an assurance that she wasn't. "For the

same reason she's not walking anywhere, the fear of being banned from the island for life." He added cryptically, "But that's about to change."

I pretended I didn't hear that either. Henry didn't have to pretend - he didn't hear it. But Julie did who glanced at me when she thought I wasn't looking.

Peter resumed, "Father is rather strict about that sort of thing. Our home is in Sydney, and as big as Sydney zoo is it is no substitute for the rainforest where animals roam wild and free. The mere thought of not coming again gives her nightmares. I've flown over this camp so many times and seen so many monkeys I was beginning to wonder if this was their home. Are they your pets?"

"No, they're my friends."

"Are they friendly by nature?"

"Not usually, only when they get to know you."

"I threw the hampers out of the helicopter," he added. "I didn't get out myself. I wasn't taking any chances. Monkeys have been known to rip people to pieces."

"Only if they've reason."

He changed the subject. "I've only had my pilot's licence a year. Landing was trickier than I thought."

"How did you know I needed a stirrup pump?" I repeated.

"Easy. I saw for myself. One time I flew low trying to catch sight of you and saw the pails, water butt and garden and put two and two together. Cora said you might live here and wanted to visit you but, as Mum said, we decided against it until we found out what you were like. I thought I'd drop a few supplies with the stirrup pump while I was about it. Hope you don't mind."

Henry and I exchanged glances.

"No, I don't mind," I said. "Six hampers is a bit over the top, don't you think?"

His expression didn't change. "I wouldn't want you to starve."

Just then Shandy appeared, sniffed around and shot back out. Moments later a baboon passed the open door with Shandy snapping at its heels. It was good, clean fun because when they passed again the baboon was snapping at Shandy's heels.

"So sweet. I could look at them all day," Julie cooed, pouring water in the sink and splashing her face to cool down. "It's certainly hot in here."

"It's hotter outside," I said.

She agreed. "We'll bring fans the next time, battery-operated"

I looked at the percolator, toaster and radio. "Isn't everything?" and carried on where we left off. "Was Cora with you when she met me?" I said.

Peter nodded. "Yes, to start with. We had been on the river most of the day, and when we saw a break in the trees we decided to stretch our legs. I didn't plan on staying long. I wanted to get back before dark." He glanced at his parents. "But you know what Cora is, as strong-headed as they come. She said she was going for walk. When she didn't come back I searched everywhere, and when I couldn't find her I settled down for the night in the cabin intending to resume the search the next morning."

I chewed on it. "What you're saying is she didn't have to spend the night with me."

"Not if she didn't want to. She would have got in touch on her mobile."

"Mobile?"

"Mobile phone. She keeps it strapped to her wrist.

She takes it everywhere she goes. She's never without it."

"Do mobiles work in rainforests?"

"They do in this rainforest."

Henry spoke up. "Cora said you spent the night under the stars."

I corrected him. "You mean under the canopy."

There was a twinkle in Julie's eye. "Did anything happen under the canopy?"

"I like to think so."

"What does Cora think?"

"Ask her." I got back to Peter. "Why didn't you phone her? I should have thought that was the first thing you'd do."

"It wouldn't have done any good," he explained. "Her mobile's in a leather case. You could ring all day and she wouldn't hear you. "

"But she did ring you."

"Not until the next morning."

"When she walked out on me?"

"If that's what she did."

"In the middle of breakfast."

"You were there. I wasn't."

"Where did she say to pick her up?"

"Further down the river. I asked her how she got there but she didn't say. It was rough going. Motor-boats aren't designed for the Grand Rapids. I got so far and she had to make it the rest of the way on her own. I managed to turn the boat round and went back the way I came. She couldn't have picked a worse spot."

"And then you both went back to Newtown?"

"That's right. I had no idea she had met you. She never tells me a thing, though she told Mum and Dad when we got back. She didn't stop talking about you."

I hadn't finished. "How far is Newtown from there?"

"Hundred miles or so. The boat does twenty-five knots. It took us four to five hours." He glanced at his parents. "Mum and Dad never come though. I'm more at home on water than in the air, but I'm learning."

Henry said, "It's been a worrying time for all."

Julie agreed parrot fashion. "Very worrying."

"You know what to do in future," I told them, "keep her away from the rainforest and to hell with nightmares."

Henry said, "And drive her insane?"

"Either that or lose her. The leopard might not be put off so easy the next time."

"And that's where you come in," Julie to me said with a smile, "You like Cora, don't you?"

"I do."

"She likes you."

"I hope so."

They looked at one another and then at me. If there is such a thing as telepathy, it was at work now. It seemed as if they had a few loose ends to clear up before they came to a final decision

Henry broke the silence. "You haven't told us why you're here."

"It's a long story."

"We're in no hurry."

*****

I told them as much as I could, omitting the deaths of Heidi, Danny and the bank robbers. Mentioning them would serve no purpose except to launch an inquiry into how they died and what part I played. And if the yacht captain got involved the inquiry would spiral out of control, and it wouldn't be my Island of Dreams any more and everything I had done would be for nothing. The adage 'let sleeping dogs lie' couldn't have been more appropriate.

I stopped. The silence was deafening.

Julie was the first to speak. "You came here to put flowers on your mother's grave, did you say?"

"That's what I said."

"How long ago?"

"A year ago, I guess."

"And you've been here ever since?"

"That's right."

"Where is the grave?"

"Two days from Newtown on foot." I noted the mingled look of shock and surprise on their faces. "Have I said something?"

Telepathy was at work again. They reminded me of the hallucin-atory figures huddled around the fire as they put their heads together. I could hear their voices but not what they were saying. I cleared the stove of ashes and put them in the ashcan for something to do.

Julie spoke again, her voice hushed, almost reverent. "Elizabeth Argyll, you say?"

"That's right. Do you know something I don't?"

"Obviously not," she replied. "You know all there is to know. The thing is Cora has been putting flowers on the grave for the past two years. The last time someone beat her to it, with orchids."

"That was me," I said, not surprised because that was the sort of thing Cora would do. I knew what they were going to say so said it for them. "What was Elizabeth doing there? That's another story."

They looked at one another again. The final decision had been made. I could only make a stab at what it was but no guesswork was needed to see it was what they considered to be in my favour.

They spread out and each did their own thing as if I wasn't there but keeping tabs on me all the same.

Henry pulled me to one side. "About the emeralds."

Before I could reply Julie said, "Didn't those four bank robbers come here, Henry, about a year ago? They killed a security guard? It was in all the newspapers."

Henry thought about it. "Didn't they catch them?"

"No, they came here, well, in this direction anyway. Their pictures were on television, in the newspapers, everywhere; a right rough-looking bunch of desperadoes if you ask me."

I cut in. "There are dozens of islands. This is the biggest. I can't see them settling here. They couldn't land because of the reefs and cliffs."

"You landed," she pointed out.

Henry came to the rescue and said my name for the first time. "Kieron obviously came in a dinghy, my dear, he is only one. There were four of them. A dinghy wouldn't hold four. One maybe, but not four."

She considered it. "Then they must be on one of the other islands."

"Yes dear."

Then she had an idea. "Shouldn't we tell the authorities? Perhaps they didn't think of looking there."

He sighed. "They looked everywhere."

She looked nervously about her as if expecting them to leap out from behind a tree. "If they're here, they might be planning to murder us this very moment."

He pacified her with good-humoured tolerance. "If they did come here they're probably dead by now, eaten by an alligator or leopard, or simply poisoned. They are a lot of ways to die if you don't know what you're doing."

"If you say so," she murmured and hurried away.

*****

Peter was over at the vegetable patch. Henry and I discussed emeralds and the possibilities of mining them once I told him where they were, albeit not the exact location. I tried to be as truthful as possible without telling a deliberate lie. I hoped to allay all thoughts of commercial gain by telling him that the crystals I had were from part of the cliff that had fallen into the sea as a result of a storm

"But there might be other veins," he argued.

"What!" I exclaimed. "And have JCBs and bulldozers uprooting trees and blowing up the mountainside, and hamburger stalls stretching as far as the eye can see? Where would be your paradise then? What would Cora say? Would Julie thank you? Trees don't grow back overnight and the blue lagoon wouldn't be blue for very long, not to mention the animals. What would happen to them? Haven't you got enough money?"

Julie came out of the cabin carrying a pail, waved in our direction and proceeded to fill it from the water butt she could barely reach from the platform I had built around it. She wasn't cut out to grow old and mellow in an ivory castle surrounded by flunkeys. If she had diamonds and pearls they were rusting away in a bank deposit box. She liked work, the harder the better, and if she got her hands dirty, so what?

Leaving Henry to mull over what I said, I helped her by placing a chock of wood under her feet so she could reach over without straining, and then helped her down the rickety steps I had also fitted. I offered to carry the pail. She wouldn't hear of it. It was touching the way she trundled to the vegetable patch where Peter was waiting, who cascaded the water the way I did by throwing it high in the air so it came down like raindrops without disturbing the soil as she went to fill another pail.

I was waiting too but she wouldn't let me help a second time. She waved me aside and filled the pail herself. Practice makes perfect and by the third journey she was carrying water as if she was born to it. Mother and son, though tired and wringing with sweat under the burning sun, were enjoying themselves.

I went back to Henry. "You were saying?"

CHAPTER TWENTY EIGHT

THE DAY AFTER

They had left the previous afternoon, and if I say life was back to normal it would be stretching it a bit. Life would never be normal, not after meeting the Bensons, who had money but didn't ram it down your throat; who maintained a comfortable lifestyle and gave to others as they would wish to be given to them. The emeralds were arranged neatly in order of size on white lace spread over a locker. Julie's handiwork. Henry didn't get to look at them, after all.

*****

Around three in the afternoon I found myself on the beach, where the civet cat had hold of the albatross and, as coincidence would have it, another albatross sat on the very rocks beyond where it took place. It was easy to imagine it was the same bird come back to thank me.

I was about to move on when, as if reading my thoughts, it preened and strutted as if showing me its fine feathers before taking to the air with a majestic sweep of its powerful wings. It circled a couple of times over the vast ocean before disappearing beneath the waves. After what seemed an eternity, it surfaced and, whether by accident or design, dropped a fish at my feet. I like to think it was the bird I saved and it was its way of saying thank you, but the fish probably struggled so much as the albatross flew over me that it let it go. Either way, I threw the fish back into the ocean and watched the bird climb the heavens until it was out of sight. Throughout, Shandy watched passively, who was by my side.

On the fringe of the trees a leopard stood ready to pounce; a leap and a bound was all the was needed, but I wouldn't advise it. Shandy wanted to tackle it on her own. I wouldn't advise that either. It disappeared into the jungle as we walked towards it. We were going through the jungle also. I had no misgivings whatsoever about being ambushed. The thought never occurred to me. I was as accustomed to the jungle as any leopard, and if it wanted a fight I would be only be too happy to oblige. But as I said, I had nothing to prove. If it left us alone, I would leave it alone.

Shandy was another matter. I had taught her as I imagined she would have been taught by her mother on how to take care of herself, but there are not many who can teach a dog when to attack and when not to attack when the blood is up. I was one of them who could.

When I told her to heel she heeled. There were no ifs and buts. As I said, discipline is the key, and I drilled it into her relentlessly, day after day to listen and obey. When the day came when she could fend for herself, I would let her do more or less as she pleased, but not before.

She had made friends with the baboons, especially the young ones while the full-grown males treated her with contempt. Of course, not all them were at the camp at the same time. Indeed, some may not have been at the camp at all, and I'll go further and say it was possible there were some I didn't even know, but they knew who I was.

I had no idea of their numbers. On that fateful day I fell through the hibiscus I estimate there were around two hundred looking down from the terrace, while no more than a dozen at a time visited the camp except when they staged a ceremony in my honour as before I set out for Elizabeth's grave when they numbered about eighty. The day-to-day basis was three or four at the most. The remarkable thing was they left the clematis alone. They went in and out without touching the fence

Maybe the camp was regarded as a kind of holiday resort and they took it in turns for a day out, or they came when they chose or in organised groups to pay their respect. Either way it was good to see them. I was surprised the young male who rebelled at not being allowed to avenge the deaths of his brethren ever visited the camp again, but he was there, and although I trusted them all, he stood out as the one least likely to hide his feelings and the one I could trust the most.

*****

I had no intention of visiting the amphitheatre again but fate decreed otherwise. The aforesaid hibiscus loomed up in front of me and the urge to visit it again was too great. I didn't fall through the hibiscus this time, instead using an opening in the floriferous as fragrant as the Garden of Eden.

There was no parade or social event this time, no bully boys slugging it out to see who could bully the most. Everything was normal with baboons going about their business calm and unhurried on the terraces and below until I turned up and then there was pandemonium.

I put my hands up to silence them. They formed a circle around me, pushing and shoving and for the first time I felt vulnerable and cursed myself for going there in the first place. Poor Shandy didn't know what to do. She was barely out of the puppy stage and more vulnerable than I was.

One stood out from the rest, a young male with staring eyes and murderous tusks. He pushed his way to the front and strutted up and down in front of me with overweening arrogance. The vengeful young male whom I had grown to trust was no place to be seen, which was just as well for there would have been a battle royal. Shandy's tail was between her legs and she whined with fear. I did my best to pacify her.

To mixed cries of applause and grunts of dissent, the baboon went up on its hind legs in a grotesque parody of a human, its twisted face and hairy legs adding pathos to burlesque. I thought about threatening it with the machete but decided against it for it might incite mob violence. Shandy and I would be crushed by sheer weight of numbers and innocent bystanders would suffer.

The circle widened into an arena, then the baboon went down on all fours and taunted me by pulling faces and screaming at the top of its voice. I feinted with my right, drawing it nearer, watching and waiting for the right moment when I could catch it was off guard, only to find it had the same idea. And that's not all. It was quicker than I thought and almost beat me at my own game. It lunged at me. I took its weight full on my chest and, dodging the slashing tusks, brought my fist across and it was all over. The crowd dispersed and Shandy and I went back the way we came.

*****

The remainder of the day was spent pottering about, cutting back the usual strands of undergrowth creeping in from the trees and watering the vegetable patch. Where the potatoes, onions and tomatoes were going from strength to strength, the carrots and other vegetables were making no progress at all. The clematis was an eye-catching ribbon of blue and pink, with splashes of red of a nectar-gathering bug whose colour proclaimed it dangerous to eat.

Next I tidied up the cabin. Not that it needed it, just a few odds and ends lying around. Julie had done a good job. It was only a short visit but she did more than two people do in a week.

*****

The baboons didn't show up until the beginning of the second week. Shandy yapped as they emerged from the trees, all three of them. I deliberately refrained from showing my customary welcome. They hung around as I went about my business and Shandy retired to her favourite spot in the shade of a tree. They took the hint and went away.

Another three days passed before they came again. This time I didn't ignore them entirely, but enough to show them I was still angry at the reception I received.

It was interesting to see the baboon that had challenged me among the visitors. I had broken his jaw and, although it had healed, it hung to one side. I caught his eye as if nothing had happened. He seemed happy with that and I couldn't care less, though if the truth were known I was glad I didn't kill him. He took me on and paid the price, like the rest.

I wasn't against their choosing another leader, all I was against was the way they did it, they could give the leadership to someone else, I didn't want it. All I wanted was to be their friend.

CHAPTER TWENTY NINE

RIVERS AND TREES

Two weeks had passed since Henry, Julie and Peter had left and I was beginning to doubt if they would return. I hoped they would, not only because I liked their company but because it was the only chance of seeing Cora again.

Life was back to normal and the baboons were free to come and go as they please, being the devoted 'watchdogs' they were I had no qualms about leaving the camp unguarded and giving Shandy a ride in the canoe. I can't count the number of times she sniffed it. She was nervous at first but soon settled down when we got going, tongue hanging out, tail wagging, watching the paddles slice through the water with monotonous regularity.

I headed east instead of west and then turned back after about a mile. I had no intention of going further, the objective being to give Shandy the feel of being on water if she were to accompany me on my travels again. It's amazing how fickle the mind can be when one minute it is so resolute in one direction, and the next floundering as it loses its way. I had definite plans, definite ideas. Now I was as lost as I ever was.

*****

Another two weeks went by. I began to despair of ever seeing Cora again. Henry and Julie struck me as honest folk true to their word but maybe, as was my habit,

I was putting too much trust in people and read into what wasn't there, or simply feeling sorry for myself.

I set about making the hammock I promised myself. First I looked around for two trees about two and half metres apart – I was two metres in height – and could find none, so made do with two joists insects had requisitioned as their home under the cabin. I sawed them to the required height, dug two holes to size, propped them upright and then packed a mixture of wet soil and pebbles around them, allowing each successive layer to dry until the compound was as hard as rock, then poured a strong glutinous resin over it and down the sides as best I could as a binding agent. Rope was a poor substitute for canvas but it was all I had. I knotted rope between the two uprights, thirty strands in all and laid a mattress on top, which slipped through the strands as soon as I lay on it.

So I plaited smaller strands the way you weave a net and it couldn't have been better. The mattress stayed where it was. It was as good a hammock as any and so comfortable I spent many afternoons doing nothing except laze in the sun watching the world go by and Shandy do her usual stuff, sniffing at everything and anything including baboons she had not seen before, who responded with good-humoured tolerance as did the older ones who had previously held her in such contempt. The younger ones were more boisterous, alternatively chasing her and she chasing them with customary tongue hanging out and tail wagging.

She was getting bigger now but no matter how big she was she would never be a match for a mature baboon. But it would never come to that. We were one big happy family and I would severely deal with any infringement that might threaten it.

I spent hours, sometimes days reflecting on what I had achieved and whether I would have attained the same degree of success if I had been someplace else. With the same guidance, resources and determination to do what I set out to do, I don't see why not. In these moods, I went about my daily chores mechanically, deep in thought. Shandy, picking up on my preoccupation, never left my side. Some of the baboons, the more perceptive ones, were extra attentive too.

*****

Shandy and I were back in the canoe heading east again. She enjoyed it as much as the last time, transfixed by the panorama as it slipped by, tail wagging, tongue sticking out. Unlike the west, this side was cluttered with trees, rainforests with hardly a break in between and no intersecting rivers to break the monotony. The one I was on had no tributaries or meanders to interrupt its flow and was monotonous to the extreme; straight as a dart, surging relentlessly towards the sea.

There were so many trees it seemed as if the ones on the banks were being pushed by the ones behind who were being pushed by the ones behind them, and so on; unlike what I was accustomed to where I could secure the canoe and stretch my legs or relax and smell the flowers and feel the breeze in my hair. I could smell the flowers and feel the breeze now but it wasn't the same, not that Shandy minded. We might have been paddling through Hades or the Sahara Desert for all she cared. It was an adventure, and like all adventures, was there to be enjoyed.

With so many trees it crossed my mind that perhaps one day there would be no trees at all in view of the speed with which they were being cut down to satisfy modern day needs, when in fact the reverse is true. Gone are the days when vast tracts of rainforests were destroyed without provision for the growth of new saplings, as seen near the pebble beach where trees were felled with no thought for tomorrow, and echoed in the yacht captain's remark: 'Pity all rainforests aren't surrounded by reefs and cliffs.'

New inroads have been made. Many of the forests are stage-managed thanks to recent progress in conservation techniques. Forests are tailored to produce appropriate-size lumber for sawmills to convert into timber, which is then used in the construction and manufacture of products familiar to us all. Nowadays, to suggest paper consumption is the reason for the loss of woodlands is as inaccurate as suggesting that increasing potato-consumption will reduce the area of potato fields. Creating the outlet for forest by-products increases the demand for paper which in turn increases areas of woodlands that can be sustained. But some logging companies are still doing it the old way; laying waste tracts of rainforests with no thought for anything or anyone except profit.

*****

There was a storm brewing. I could feel it in my bones. Not that it would affect us. The canopy is nature's umbrella, which made me wonder how the trees and other plants survived without water until I recalled rainforests, by their very nature, get the most rain of all. It spills, seeps and trickles through the canopy refreshing everything in its path.

I turned the canoe around and went back the way we came. The water was smooth and fast with hardly a ripple. Shandy loved it. Once or twice she snarled and kicked her back legs when a bird perched on the bow or a leaf fell from the branches above, but all in all she was well behaved.

*****

Back in camp I busied myself keeping the jungle at bay, watering the vegetable patch and carrying out the usual jobs that had to be done no matter how unimportant they might seem.

For some unknown reason the baboons stopped coming as they had done before. I was accustomed to their moods and knew how capricious and unpredictable they could be but I couldn't explain this part of their behaviour. It wasn't anything I had done. They just stopped what they were doing as if by a pre-arranged signal and shot off through the trees. Still, I can't complain. They asked for nothing and gave me everything in return.

It takes months, sometimes years, sometimes never to get close to a baboon without feeling the wrath of those terrible tusks, and there I was, not only accepted as an important member of the troop but also revered as leader. They came to me for protection yet they protected me. This coupled with acceptance into the hierarchy of the rainforest must surely be every naturalist's dream. I didn't ask for it, I didn't aspire to it, I didn't even think about it. I just happened to be in the right place at the right time.

CHAPTER THIRTY

IN CONCLUSION

At the beginning of the third week since Henry's, Julie's and Peter's departure, I made a surprising discovery. The bamboo fence started to grow. What strange manner of propagation was this; without preparation, without tilling, and for the most part without water for I was too intent on seeing to the needs of the vegetable crop without wasting time attending to something I didn't want to grow and thought would never grow?

*****

Shandy was lost without the baboons. She had no one to play with; boredom was setting in so I gave her more freedom to explore more of the camp and the surrounding area. She knew how far to go and when to come back home.

During those weeks I spent a great deal of time walking up and down when not carrying out my daily routine. I couldn't stand still. One time I was watering the vegetable patch when it rained and I kept on watering deliberately getting soaked to the skin to give me something to do getting dry.

One afternoon I thought I heard a helicopter. I looked up and all could see was clear blue sky. Melancholy was setting in. I shrugged it off.

*****

I went down to the river and Shandy came with me. She barely left my side now the baboons were no longer about. When they returned she would be up to her old tricks again, teasing, yapping, running away.

I sat where Henry had sat and passed the time trying to fathom why he wanted emeralds to add to his millions unless it was something to say while we got better acquainted. He was the friendly type. They were all friendly; it's just that I took him the wrong way, that's all. I should have known he didn't mean anything. It was the word 'dump' I didn't like or maybe the way he said it. It sounded condescending, patronising. But I apologised and there was no ill feeling.

Then Julie came to mind. Good old Julie. Cora had a lot of her mannerisms, indeed, that is how I imagined Julie to be when she was Cora's age, only Julie wasn't fond of the jungle, leastways, not that I know of. But she was getting old. Maybe if she had been younger ... Who knows?

Peter was a stiff upper lip type devoted to his sister who would go through hell and to high water to see she came to no harm. And he was clever if not a little careless sometimes. I couldn't fly a helicopter or handle a motorboat. He could. It took me all my time to drive a car.

Barks and coughs heralded the return of the baboons. Shandy pricked up her ears and went to meet them. There were five in all, a conciliatory force sent to gauge my mood and see if we were pals again. Of course we were. I didn't send them away in the first place. I just wanted to teach them a lesson, that's all.

Significantly, among their members was the last one I expected to conciliate on any matter, and that was the one who took me on, the one with the broken jaw.

*****

I heard the helicopter again. It was getting nearer. The baboons forgot their mission and made for the trees along with everything else that could run, fly or leap. Then it came into view, only this time it missed the trees and hovered with a tremendous downdraft before touching down as gently as before.

I went to meet Henry, Julie and Peter. They were different than the last time when they didn't know what to expect. The only animal present was Shandy who greeted them with wagging tail and friendly growls. Julie bent down and stroked her. We retired to the cabin. They seemed happy enough but something was under the surface.

Peter was bursting at the seams to tell me what was wrong. Exhorting him to calm down, I lit the stove and put the kettle on. We all sat down.

"You handle the helicopter very well," I said, "better than the last time. Spit it out. What is it?"

Peter thanked me and began. "We've been following Cora for the past week."

"What do you mean, follow!" I exclaimed. "This is a rainforest, not Piccadilly Circus."

He said, "She's taken the motor-boat. When we told her where we had been she insisted on seeing you herself. Father told her there were things to do first but she wouldn't listen and took the boat anyway. We chased after her in the helicopter."

It sounded so funny I felt like laughing. "You didn't catch her then."

He shook his head. "No place to land. She took the river map. She knew where she was going. Four hundred miles is a long way, especially when you can hardly see who you're following. The rivers don't help. They wind and turn and disappear and come back God knows where. She was doing twenty knots, six hours a day mooring up at night and wasn't easy to follow. We had to land in some awkward places and pick up where we left off the following morning. It was either rest up or blow up. Even helicopters have to rest some times, and they're not the most comfortable places to sleep in. Some mornings she had a thirty miles start. We've been travelling seven days without proper sleep."

Henry yawned. "And don't I know it. I'm stiff all over."

It got funnier. "Didn't she run out of fuel?" I said.

"No such luck. There's a reserve tank and I always keep extra on board. It was us who almost ran out of fuel. We had to return to Newtown."

I wanted to smile. "What about food? She does eat, doesn't she?"

"She can live on berries." He checked his watch. "She should be here within the hour if I can stay awake that long."

I ran out of questions.

Julie followed Henry's example and yawned too, "Me too. I'll be glad when this is all over. I've got a lot to say to that girl."

"Until then," I said, "get some sleep. We're not short of beds. Take your pick."

"Not until I know Cora is safe," she told me.

The kettle boiled and she made the tea, surprised that I only had powdered milk. "You take this in your tea, Kieron!"

It was the first time she had said my name and it sounded nicer than when Henry said it. "It's all I have," I replied.

Henry and Peter didn't seem to mind, who drank theirs and asked for more. Julie gave them more. I had another cup too. Julie just had the one.

"I'll do the dinner when Cora arrives," she announced, "then we can have dinner together. What have we got, Kieron?"

I opened the food cupboard and several tins fell out.

She picked one up. "Baked beans," and put it on the table. "Any ham?"

I found a tin of ham.

"Beans and ham it is then." She announced, proceeded to empty the cupboard, put each item back in its rightful place, stood back to admire her handiwork and busied herself dusting and cleaning to pass the time.

*****

There was a commotion outside. We went to see what was going on. Shandy had upset a male baboon and was running for her life. Julie screamed as I shouted at the top of my voice. The baboon stopped in its tracks. Shandy kept on running right into Julie's arms. I went over to the baboon and offered apologies on Shandy's behalf to prove there were no favourites despite the fact that Shandy slept in the cabin. I'm sure if the truth be known Shandy had teased once too often and the baboon had had enough. Normally they all behaved themselves inside the camp, including Shandy with whom I remonstrated to show I wasn't pleased. The baboon, seemingly satisfied, sauntered off through the trees.

"I said you were an amazing man," Julie said.

They retuned to the cabin. I made my excuses and made my way to the river. Birds were perched on the helicopter's rotor blades and an assortment of rodents was sniffing around. The baboons were nowhere to be seen, Shandy neither, who was probably sulking in the shade of a tree.

*****

This part of the river was too shallow for a motor-boat, but there was a way through if you knew where to go, and Cora knew where to go because she had the map. But she wanted to go no place except here. What she didn't know was I would be waiting.

I sat on the grass bank, and a voice came to me like a voice in a dream. "Kieron, I miss you. I will always miss you." I looked around. There was no one there. I was seized by panic and wanted to run and keep on running. Then, as suddenly I was calm and as in control as I would ever be.

The purr of an engine rose above the other sounds. I sat up and couldn't believe my eyes when the sleek contours of a motor-boat came into view. It hugged the middle of the river sending up waves of foam in its wake. Then it swept into the side and slewed to a halt just short of the shelf that jutted like a reef beneath the surface.

Cora came out of the cabin and threw me a rope, which I secured to a tree. Then she ducked through the deck rail and jumped. I caught her. A great feeling of happiness surged through me as we kissed and kept on kissing as if we had known each other all our lives, and a lifetime had passed since we last saw each other. I held her perhaps tighter than I should but she didn't complain. Indeed, her small muscular frame responded with equal vigour, her writhing body asking for more. We sank slowly and inexorably to the grass beneath our feet.

*****

Birds still perched on the rotor blades of the helicopter and rodents still sniffed around. The only difference being baboons converged from all directions, even Shandy put in an appearance.

Cora clung to my arm. "For God's sake, Kieron, what manner of place is this? Peter's here, are Mummy and Daddy?" A flush crawled up her throat and her voice dropped to a whisper. "Where are they?" she repeated.

"They are safe and sound," I assured her.

The baboons grouped together, mumbling under their breath, not knowing what to make of Cora who, as far as they were concerned, was showing undue familiarity by holding my hand. I took her to meet them. Her apprehension increased as we got nearer and she would have run away if I had let her.

The baboons didn't move. I singled out the mother and baby I had previously held and took the baby in my arms again. The mother went up on her hind legs like a dog, her expression uncannily human; her eyes deep, feeling and intelligent. She took the baby back with a tenderness unthinkable in one generally conceived as clumsy and brutish. I smiled. Mothers are mothers no matter what shape or form. Shandy, as usual, stuck her tongue out and wagged her tail.

Cora looked on with a mixture of incredulity and surprise. "Your dog?" she queried.

"They are all mine," I replied.

"You're a lucky man."

I squeezed her shoulders. "I am now."

"You were taking me to Mummy and Daddy?" she reminded me.

*****

The cabin had that homely feeling. Soft music from the radio played in the background. Windows were open and the fussiness of Julie shone in every corner. Nothing was out of place. The fans Julie had mentioned kept the air cool and for the first time it felt like a real home.

Peter was sound asleep. On another bed Henry was sleeping too, with Julie by his side. It was too much. Tears rolled down Cora's cheeks.

"Aren't they lovely?" she said. "Haven't I got a nice family?"

I looked at each in turn. "I think so."

She spotted the emeralds and ran over like a little girl. "Whose are these?"

I went up close. "Yours."

She turned and faced me. "Where did you get them?"

I looked into her upturned eyes. She was no longer vulnerable, crying inside. Her teeth were still dreams to smile with like she was smiling now. We kissed and kissed again ...

THE END